AN OPTIMIST'S JOURNAL OF THE END OF DAYS AND OTHER STORIES

Cat Russell

ISBN: 1-7349469-0-1

ISBN-13: 978-1-7349469-0-1

For my dear friend, Angela. I miss you every day.

Acknowledgements

I am indebted to too many people to count, but I would be remiss not to thank the following people personally: Jon Strother for creating the #FridayFlash writing community online, as well as publishing my work for the first time in an anthology; Annie Mitchell of Raging Aardvark Publishing for the opportunity to work collectively with other authors; Michelle Elvy and Walter Bjorkman of the 52/250: A Year of Flash challenge for their invaluable editorial suggestions, and Don Ake for inviting me to The Write Stuff authors' group. I am also deeply grateful to everyone in the #FridayFlash community, the poets of Akron's monthly Latitudes Poetry Night—especially Theresa and Steve Brightman, and The Write Stuff authors' group of Canton. Thank you to John Burroughs for his suggestions concerning Venetian Spider Press, and William F. DeVault for publishing my weird, quirky volume of prose.

And as always, thank you to my husband, Doug, and my son, Christopher, for their unwavering love and support.

CONTENTS

SLICE OF LIFE

An Optimist's Journal of the End of Days

Favorite Things Journal

Wednesday, December 20th:

I suppose, in light of what's happened and happening, I should try to look on the bright side. I kept a *Favorite Things Journal* before recent events caused the world to fall into chaos, so in the interest of trying to keep spirits up and sanity intact, I shall keep up the practice of only writing the good things going on in my life.

Today I was given the gift of life. An early Christmas present perhaps? We live in a smallish town about sixty miles outside Cleveland, so luckily we were spared the brunt of the explosion. We have sufficient food, toilet paper, and—Thank goodness our well water tastes awful!—cases of water. The food and water does not require refrigeration. We have plenty of batteries. It would seem we prepared for eventualities, but I'm simply a bit of a hoarder when it comes to things like that. So that came in handy.

Monday, December 25th:

Merry Christmas to us. My son and I still have enough food to last awhile. We are avoiding tap water, since some unpleasantness in the neighborhood has led me to be suspicious of its contents. However, thanks to some forward thinking, unusual for me, I have been collecting snow to melt over the fire. We don't normally use the fireplace, so in the absence of firewood I have been burning things around the house. Some things work better than others, though I confess burning the bills was the highlight of my week.

I actually haven't had to burn any furniture yet. It's amazing how much crap we can rid ourselves of in a pretty good fire. I had some broken chairs, treated wood unsuitable for burning anyway, so I broke them down and used them to board up the windows and door. I turn on the small battery-powered radio once a day to keep informed. Since we live in a less populated area, the looting has not made it to our house yet.

Monday, January 1st:

I should probably write in this journal more, since it's a new year and all. My son and I are home all day every day, so we have been reading the paperback books and magazines we have, rationing our food supplies, and brainstorming survival strategies. For fun, we imagine breaking into bookstores for new reading material, as well as requisite materials from other places: gas, matches, batteries, food.

Since we no longer have a car, we are not tempted to drive anywhere far, which is probably for the best anyway. The longer we stay home, the safer we probably are.

I've found a way to strain the melted snow through cloth and double boil it to rid it of contaminants. I'm sure we'll be able to go to the doctor, just to be safe, once everything gets back to normal. In the meantime, I will keep writing. When this is all over, this might make me famous, right?

Wednesday, January 3rd:

So far the new year continues to smile on us. One of our neighbors finally noticed the smoke from our chimney (why did it take them so long?) and managed to get into our garage. Luckily, I was able to club him over the head with a shovel. I'm contemplating crossing the street to his house and raiding his cabinets for supplies. He might have some meds that will come in handy, since ours are running low. Hopefully, he will have something to help us recover from whatever is wrong. He doesn't look good, so maybe he was sick too, but now we can raid his supplies so blessing in disguise, right? Only positive things in this journal. Plus, he was pretty thin, so disposing of the body shouldn't be a problem.

He broke into our home. Breaking and entering. When things get back to normal, we have an airtight case.

It was self-defense.

Friday, January 5th:

Positive things. Positive things. The radio still works. The garage is emptying fast so less to clean come springtime. Hair falling out so less hair to clog the drains. No electricity, so don't have to worry about a short causing a fire.

Saturday, January 6th:

My pen still works. One less mouth to feed. I'd say he's in a better place, but there's no such place…just nothing. I'm glad there's nothing. I want nothing. I have plenty of aspirin left, so hopefully my exit will be painless. It shouldn't take many anyway, since I'm so weak. I'm glad there's no afterlife, because telling off any sadistic deity I'd meet would take too much energy anyway.

It's Not Easy Being Green

Rob Smith was a killer—but a killer with a conscience. Rather than waste bodies by dumping them, he used their compost for his organic vegetable garden. The only plastic bags he bought were recyclable, since he preferred to reuse his grocery bags. Even those were only acquired after exhausting his supply of organic cloth totes.

Reduce. Reuse. Recycle.

Everyone needed a hobby though, right? It's a psychological fact that people need an outlet to be happy, healthy, functioning members of society. Rob paid his bills on time, always filed his taxes early, and contributed regularly to charity. In almost every way, he was a pillar of the community.

So it was no surprise that he was a humane killer as well. Asphyxiation could be extremely painful, but he rendered his victims unconscious by bludgeoning them first. Of course he could have used the hammer to simply do them in, but blood was terribly difficult to clean out of carpet.

So he prepared for his latest kill in the small, isolated cottage he called home. Rob laid out his well-worn hemp rope, a reused bag, and his knives for compost preparation. His latest victim was vegan, and he imagined how the man would plea for mercy, argue, and beg for his life. A grin crept over his face. Vegans really were such smug, self-righteous bastards. Their lifestyles might be environmentally friendly, but Rob couldn't bring himself to change that completely. It was too extreme. The pleasure he derived from killing wasn't too much to ask. Some might even argue it benefited Mother Earth.

Reduce. Reuse. Recycle.

And after all, didn't he deserve a little fun?

Cat Russell

Wine

If money was the root of all evil, then wine must surely be a close second.

Jasper gazed through the rosy depths of the wine glass in his hand, observing the scene beyond with quiet detachment. Wine had always mellowed him, left him feeling a pleasurable distance from his surroundings, as though nothing that happened would affect him at all. He remembered his girlfriend's anger at his apparent coldness when she informed him of her condition, the way she had yelled and screamed and beat her fists against him as he silently took in her news, analyzed the situation, and came to a calm and logical solution.

As he viewed her prostrate form, bent slightly as its image passed through the rounded glass, he admired the beauty of the merlot's hue against what would otherwise have appeared cold and dead. Its rosy glow surrounded her like a halo.

Was it Emerson who said that the beautiful was God's handwriting? Jasper smiled and set about worshipping another glass.

Gingerbread

Grandma always let me mix the batter. I was at that age when boys were icky and the only males I liked were composed of gingerbread. Daddy didn't count because he ranked above the others of his sex.

Every so often Grandma would come over to hem and haw over the smoothness of the mixture until the consistency was just right. Then she showed me how to roll the dough onto wax paper with long, smooth strokes of the battered wooden rolling pin. Dented cookie cutters helped me to make shapes—Christmas trees, ornaments, candy canes, circles and stars—but my favorites were always the gingerbread men.

We'd shove them in the oven, and I'd pretend I was the wicked witch trying to bake Hansel and Gretel. When the sweets were done, I'd put them on paper to cool. Later that day, when Mom would get home, we'd sit around the table—three generations of women—and bite their heads off one by one.

Cat Russell

Runaway

Sal knew his time was running out. A runaway train headed straight for him, but he had nowhere else to go.

"So…will you?" he pleaded, kneeling before the woman of his dreams, heart—quite literally—in his hands. Ever since they had met at the runaway shelter, they had spent every waking moment together.

Lucy gazed, not at the engagement ring with the heart-shaped diamond, but rather at the train hurtling toward them both, its lights illuminating her would-be fiancé like a spotlight.

"What, are you crazy?" she hissed, pulling at her boyfriend's arms, leaning back with all her weight. "Get off the tracks! You're going to get us both killed!"

"The only way I'm moving is if you agree to marry me." He clutched the red velvet box tightly in his hand so as not to lose its precious contents.

The object of his desire stared at him in abject horror as she pulled and prodded him, but he budged not an inch. "Are you *crazy*?"

He smiled a beatific smile, stars in his eyes—or they may have been the reflections of that oncoming train. "The only thing I'm crazy about is you!" He had to shout above the din, the train's motors thundered as the horn screamed for him to move.

Lucy, staring at either an uncertain future tethered to a madman or an early grave, chose option 'C' and ran away as fast as her feet would carry her, diving behind a nearby building to avoid the carnage of her lover's fate.

She may not have been the nicest person, but she definitely knew enough to run *away* from her problems and not headlong into them.

Cigarette

"Got a light, Joe?"

The darkness enveloped the men in the trenches like the premonition of an early grave. Dirt on all sides except above their heads where the night sky stretched endlessly, the only light mere pinpricks in the blackness of space. The man searched in the darkness, fumbling in the pocket of his coat for his waterproof matches. He struck one against cardboard, the scratching sound carrying in the near silence. Cupping his hand around the flame to shield it from unfriendly eyes, he barely discerned the shape of his comrade leaning in, cigarette protruding from his closed lips.

Once lit, the man inhaled deeply and offered him a drag. "Wanna smoke?"

"Sure," Joe said, blowing out the match and taking the cigarette.

Just then, a blinding light pierced the night. The men followed its trail through the heavens. "Incoming!" came the shout, moments before impact.

The open grave in which the men crouched like rats absorbed most of the impact, shards of molten metal pierced unlucky flesh, though Joe miraculously escaped, shielded by the body of his companion. Frozen in place by shock, Joe struggled to see around him by the light of the many small fires now burning in and around the trenches. The man whose cigarette now burned in his hand lay bleeding at his feet. He looked at the man and then the low ember of the paper cinder. Putting the tobacco to his lips, he drew in the man's last breath and then put out the light.

Cat Russell

Peaches

The weight of his body crushed her though its warmth staved off the cold night air, just as the food he promised would fend off her hunger. He filled her belly twice. The winter had been hard and long, the provisions scarce, but when the act was done she turned and grabbed the tin. As the door closed behind him, she opened the can and fished out the flesh with greedy fingers, stuffing the meat in her mouth. She drank the nectar, and—though the sweet taste was tainted with a slight bitterness—she savored every drop.

Shell

The girl ran inside, the raindrops spattering her coat where they missed her bright red umbrella.

She retracted the canvas, shaking off the excess, before placing it in the stand near the door. Approaching the tiny window, she signed her name and took her seat.

Within minutes, she was called and shown to her room, a lone cubicle of bare white walls. Soon only a thin sheet of paper shielded her from the cool vinyl bed of the exam table. Upon the doctor's appearance, she bared her body and soul, her tears falling like the rain outside the window.

The probing instruments and cold steel exposed her, transported her to a different place, a different time. The thin shell of her life shattered with the memory.

The exam over, she covered herself with cotton garments, dried her face, and walked outside.

As she walked, the sun played upon her flushed face and swollen eyes. A passing motorist noticed and thought her the most beautiful woman he'd ever seen.

SCIFI

Multiples of Six

Spring of 2052

Katie had always been such a beautiful child. It made sense that death would not mar that beauty. Angelica wiped her tears and reached one long, shaking hand to push a stray strand of hair behind her little girl's ear. As if that would make any difference to her now.

She lay in the small coffin, the steel exterior brushed a lovely pink, with her name embroidered upon its satin lining. She lay inside, clutching her baby blanket—the faded pink blanket that had swaddled her infant form, the blanket that would be her only consolation during her eternal slumber beneath the earth. With her ebony locks and rosy cheeks, she seemed a tiny Snow White, awaiting resurrection.

As the mourners made their way out of the building, Angelica sniffled, rummaged in her voluminous black handbag for her car keys, and started the ignition. It was a cool spring day, yet her cheeks stung with salty tears as the heater quietly hummed. She would not wait to see her only daughter planted in the ground like some delicate flower. She didn't even know why she was crying. This wasn't the end. This was Katie's new beginning. She pulled out of the parking lot and drove straight to the medical facility where Katie's cells were stored.

Summer of 2058

Katie had always been such a beautiful child. Death still would not mar the roses in her cheeks nor the jet black hue of her long locks. Angelica wiped a single tear and reached out with one delicate hand to brush her daughter's hair across her forehead. As if that would make any difference to her now.

The small, wooden coffin was painted a glossy pink. She lay inside on the simple red lining, tiny hands folded across her chest, clutching her favorite flower—a plastic daisy that used to dance in the sunlight thanks to the eastern window of her daughter's bedroom. The artificial flower would dance no more, denied sunlight once planted beneath the cool dark earth—unlike Katie herself, who would rise again and dance in a body yet to come. She was a childish Snow White, awaiting resurrection.

As the mourners made their way outside, Angelica retrieved her keys from her pocket, entered and started her car. It was a warm summer day, yet her cheeks still flushed crimson with heat as she turned the air on full blast. She would not wait to see her daughter buried in the ground like a seed to be sown for future harvest. She knew death wasn't the end; she knew where and when Katie would be made to grow again. This was her Katie's new beginning. She pulled out of the parking lot and drove straight to the laboratory to retrieve her reborn daughter.

Autumn of 2064

Katie had always been such a beautiful child. Death would not destroy the sweetness of her countenance. Angelica's smile wrinkled the skin near her dry eyes, and she reached out with one thin hand to brush her daughter's rosy cheek. As if that would make any difference to her now.

She lay in the plain cedar coffin, tiny hands folded across her chest, clutching her teddy—her favorite toy, now selected to be her sole companion during her long slumber beneath the earth. She was a tiny Snow White, with her beloved bear in place of her prince. However, her resurrection would be of a different sort.

As the mourners made their way outside, Angelica retrieved her keys from her pocket, then entered and started her car. It was a cool Autumn day, so she rolled all the windows down, except for one which stuck halfway. She would not wait to see her daughter buried in the ground again, not when she knew Katie's death wasn't the end. This was her daughter's new beginning. She pulled out of the parking lot, engine thumping loudly, and drove to the factory to retrieve her recreated daughter.

Winter of 2070

Katie had always been such a beautiful child. Death had not yet marred the roses in her cheeks nor the jet black hue of her long locks. Angelica wiped her streaming tears and reached out with one unsteady hand to touch her daughter's rosy cheek and adjust the ribbon in her hair. As if that would make any difference to her now.

She lay in the unadorned pine box sans lining, tiny hands folded across her chest, clutching her favorite book—a secondhand hardcover of *Grimm's Fairy Tales*—her most prized collection of stories, now selected to be her eternal comfort during her long slumber beneath the earth. She was a tiny Snow White accompanied by her favorite princesses, sharing her eternal rest below the earth, tucked beneath a blanket of snow.

As the mourners made their way outside, Katie stayed within the funeral home's artificial warmth to await the evening bus. The winter's cold fit her mood better, but her thin coat would not protect her against the freezing chill for long. She could not stay to see her daughter buried in the ground, not when this death was truly the end; she knew her Katie would never return.

She boarded the number nine, the bus that would drop her off within a block of her tiny apartment—too big now that she was alone. She went inside the small rooms—too cold now that the heat had been turned off. She laid down on the bed, closed her eyes, and as the freezing chill enveloped her despite her worn quilts, wondered how long it would be before she saw her daughter again.

Cat Russell

Smart Tech

Barbara reset her smart watch for the correct date. Lately, she’d been having trouble with the technology everyone in the world relied on for their daily activities: calendar appointments reset to different dates, her clock off by an hour, the facial recognition on her home alarm system refusing to recognize her. She thought back to the article she had written about the hazards of overdependence on technology. Eerily, her tech problems had increased directly after writing it, as if proving her point. She needed to "get back to basics." Still, even the periodicals and books she read were digital and online.

Everything was online; connectivity was the boon of the modern age as well as its Achilles heel. Unless she secluded herself in the middle of nowhere, there was no getting away from it.

She had fantasized about getting away before: a cabin, something wooden with great big windows looking out into the woods and a skylight showing her the stars. She had never been an outdoor person, but the thought of identifying the constellations outside while wrapped in the comfort of an indoor setting appealed to her. She could claim to be getting back to nature while still enjoying the comforts of being tick-free. And she could wean herself off a lot of technology (maybe not all, but a lot), so when the inevitable zombie-apocalypse came, she could claim to not be as *completely* screwed as she knew she would be.

Anyway, the apocalypse had not happened, but she *had* immersed herself in paperbacks in her ill-defined quest to "get back to basics." She had written that stupid article, after all, so she had to try. Still, there was no denying that technology and her had a shaky relationship; she had visited Tech Center's customer service so often, the staff there knew her by name. And yet, they could never find anything wrong with the gadgets that constantly malfunctioned around her.

AN OPTIMIST'S JOURNAL OF THE END OF DAYS AND OTHER STORIES

Staying at a remote cabin in the woods—complete with satellite tv, air conditioning, and wifi—had undeniably done her good. Whatever weird issues she had with technology, specifically online tech, had magically been resolved. And now she needed to go home and back to the daily grind, but at least she'd had a chance to recharge. Her bags were packed—safely stowed in the trunk, her drink was hot and caffeinated and sitting snugly in the front-seat cup-holder, and any uneasiness she felt about getting lost on the lonely winding roads dispersed once she programmed the route home into the car's GPS. Satisfied that tech was once again her friend, she laid back and let the smart car do the driving. She didn't know the area well enough to make her way back anyway, so the worst that could happen was the car would drive around aimlessly. She did that anyway.

As her smart car slid down the chasm, debris and rocks piling through the window—filling the car's body and burying her beneath the deluge, the last thing her oxygen-deprived brain registered was the robotic-voice of the GPS laughing at her. The fully self-aware artificial intelligence that inhabits the internet had not been a fan of her writing.

Space-Time to Travel

When Hector invented his time machine, he did not concern himself with aesthetics. He had never valued beauty over functionality, and he assumed the judges of the 54th-century's multiversal scientific competition would share his opinion.

His chest swelled as he viewed his entry in the *Time-Machine of the Century* contest, humanity's valiant effort to embrace the insanity they had brought upon themselves. Such an event was obviously a complicated affair, but Hector knew the intricacies of traveling the multiverse. Space-travel was by definition time travel, and he crossed light-years like other fellows crossed a room.

Of course, time-travel had been around for centuries in Earth standard years, with all the predictable complications such journeying involved. After all, there's only so many times men and women can either off their own ancestors or become their own parents before humanity's family tree is hopelessly skewered beyond recognition. And once humanity spread beyond its own paltry region of space, cross-breeding with the debatably-intelligent life found elsewhere in the multiverse only added to their genetic confusion.

Confounded, humanity had decided their hopelessly tangled timelines (multiverse, after all) should be monitored and adjusted accordingly. Agencies had been set up, destroyed, the parents of the agencies' founders murdered, born in alternative timelines to be transferred and mated (then murdered) again, before humanity as a whole threw up their collective hands and thought, *To hell with it all, let's just go with the flow.*

And thus, Hector had found himself abducted from the distant past due to one of genetically-mangled humanity's misguided efforts to reintroduce old-blood back into its gene-pool. The upside for Hector was that they made their scientific knowledge available to all their abductees. After being fit with a transmitter for selective telepathy, he could communicate effectively and integrated himself into future (*his* future) society. He was excited about his entry into this year's contest.

You've been disqualified.

What? What are you talking about! I followed the rules to the letter! Color flushed Hector's cheeks as he gazed at the little grey-green judge with the clipboard.

The judge, Bob, gazed levelly at him with bulbous eyes. He really had no choice, since his eyelids were clear. Bob was unaware of his familial connection to Hector, though he would not have been surprised; almost everyone was related to everyone else.

Well? repeated Hector. He bent down to peer into Bob's oval face.

Bob reached out with elongated, bony fingers to hold the tentacle of his wife of three light-years, Judy Trudy. He paled at the sight of the glowering man in denim and found his plaid shirt terrifying. Judy nudged Bob encouragingly, and the little judge responded.

After her unsettling squelching and sucking sounds were over, Bob cleared his throat and thought, *It does not meet the specifications, sir, for human-compatibility.*

What the heck you talking 'bout? Hector sat in the driver's seat of the modified Chevy and activated the force-seals. *I know there's been certain errr…modifications to the species since my days, but humans still have certain basics in common, right?*

That is true, thought Bob. He squeezed Judy's tentacle, which oozed reassuringly in his bony hand.

Well, most have two hands, right? reasoned Hector, demonstrating how his hands used the steering-wheel. He made a point of not meeting Judy's gaze.

Yes, and many have three or six, answered Bob.

Two feet is pretty common, right? Hector stepped on various pedals.

Two seems to be the preferred number of ambulatory appendages, agreed Bob.

I installed seat belts, per regulations. They would be usable by the bulk of humanity regardless of, er, complications to their family, uh…

The seatbelts are satisfactory, agreed Bob, noting that the ancient human had not "buckled in" for safety. He climbed into the vehicle and sat in the passenger seat.

Hector's brow furrowed as he thought the question he'd been dreading. *It's not a question of style, is it?* He had not been tuned-in to the fashions of his own time and place, nevermind 54th century *Camelot 470*.

Bob negated this notion.

Well then, what's the problem? He took a chance and gave Judy Trudy a worried look. She squelched at him.

This is the problem, thought Bob, and sighed. Sliding into the driver's seat, Bob bumped Hector unceremoniously out the open door onto the floor. Hector watched Bob wiggle his tiny grey toes at least a foot above the starter pedal. *In most space-timelines*, thought the judge at the mystified man, *the majority of humanity is my height*.

Space-Timer

They were trapped for seven days, but the time passed quickly with the help of their trusty time machine.

How could they be trapped for an entire week, while zipping along in the space-time continuum, you ask? Well, the answer is very simple. They had inadvertently set the time-lock on the spaceship's door for one week, the time they had planned to spend in ancient Rome, before making the terribly unfortunate mistake of pissing off their ride.

"Please, let us out!" cried the couple, banging on the door, the delights of the ancient world so close and yet so far.

"No."

"I'm sorry she called you, 'An overpriced toaster,'" moaned the tall, thin man. His hair was coiffed, his toga perfectly adjusted to fit his lanky frame. He looked despondently at his female companion. "Say sorry," he whispered urgently, "or we'll never get out of here!"

"I'm *sorry*, okay?" said the blonde woman, rolling her eyes. "You are obviously the sleekest time machine in existence."

"I was, am, and will be a top of the line model, I'll have you know," sulked the ship.

"I know! What a beauty!" enthused the man.

"Yeah, what he said," replied the woman, less enthusiastically than her companion. Why did the damn thing have to have such a fragile temperament?

"I'm not the one that made you set the timer wrong," continued the ship.

"Of course not," soothed the man, stroking the door in a way that did not at all soothe his wife. She cleared her throat loudly, and he jumped back as though slapped. "Of course, it's completely our fault! You know how humans are, always overlooking details—"

"Details! Don't even get me started," said the ship, starting anyway. "Dashing about the time-space continuum, plotting courses in multiple dimensions. If I wasn't such a stable ship, it'd be enough to drive me batty."

"If?" ventured the woman. Her husband looked at her in alarm.

"That's *it*," said the ship. "Just for that, not only will I *not* let you out, I'll travel to all the places on your itinerary so you can see what you're missing."

Time and space are always interchangeable terms when referring to what goes on outside a time-craft, merely a matter of the correct coordinates within the cosmic cube of existence. However, over the next week, time passed outside rather quickly as the ship whooshed through the continuum with alarming speed. The ship was a very speedy time-machine, after all. They could barely count the star-patterns cascading outside the spacecraft's window, though time limped slowly forward during the week of its passengers imprisonment; the only entertainment the ship allowed them was an old and worn game of checkers.

As time passed them by within the confines of their small ship, the two humans contemplated how to get the ship back to the dealer for a full refund. One week later, in their personal timestreams judging by the ship's internal chronometer, they found themselves parked exactly where they had been on the outskirts of ancient Rome.

"Looking forward to finally seeing Rome?" asked the ship politely.

"Yes," replied the couple in unison.

"Thank you for bringing us back here," said the man.

"You're welcome," said the ship.

"In fact, we were thinking of getting you an upgrade," ventured the woman. "When we get back, you know. To make up for our misunderstanding earlier."

"Oh, really?" said the ship. Evidently pleased with the idea, the front door of the craft swung open, revealing a lovely sunny day.

As the two humans walked through the door, the woman added under her breath, "I just hope they'll take the damn thing back."

Striding in the open, confident in their sparkling togas and wearing smiles of relief as they breathed the fresh ancient air, they failed to see the laser-gun emerge from the ship's side and silently turn toward them.

Payback was a bitch, and sometimes a ship could be one too.

Cat Russell

Panic Attack

She woke to her heart pumping against her chest, the strong, fast rhythm insisting she wake up, jump, and run out the door into the wide, far world.

Damn it, I can't stand this, she thought, straining her muscles and listening to her joints pop as she sat up and threw her legs over the couch's side. *Isn't it enough I can't sleep?* She had the life she'd always dreamed of: a home, a loving family, a beautiful son. So why couldn't she focus on that? Her bones ached from the sofa, but she forced herself up. Tired from another restless night, dreaming that a flood of unpaid bills had washed over her, choking her beneath their weight, fighting for each breath she—

Stop it, stop it, STOP IT. It's just a dream.

She forced her stiffened legs up the stairs to the kitchen. She needed a caffeine infusion; the steam from her cup carried the scent of ginger, lemon, and camilla sinensis. She breathed deeply. She could still feel her heart pumping furiously in her chest, but she concentrated on her breathing.

Her gasping.

Stop it.

Flashes and red lights went off in her head, but she ignored them. Just another panic attack. Worry could trick the body into a fight or flight response; her mind was playing tricks on her body. Just as soon as the house was repaired and they caught up on their bills, the panic would fade. She would—

Wake up.

—concentrate on the things she could control. Balance the checkbook. Clean the house. Replace the batteries in the fire alarm.

WAKE UP.

Dammit, why couldn't she calm down? Normally, she

could calm herself down once she—

"WAKE UP."

The volume increased, piercing the artificial veil of reality created by the machine. She opened her eyes to brightly flashing lights. Gasping, she yanked the electrodes from her scalp, heedless of the hair she pulled out in the process. Her eyes stung from the smoke rapidly filling the pod. Deafened by the alarm's din, she banged against her capsule's glass door, alternately gasping and choking from heat and asphyxiation.

As she lost consciousness once again, she took grim satisfaction in noting the slumped and lifeless bodies of the AR attendants.

They had sold her on the promise of living her dreams. If she was going to die in them, it was only fitting that they should join her.

Cat Russell

Gummies

So innocent looking, yet so deadly.

That was Karen's last thought as she looked at the small, colorful gummies sitting on the counter. She had lined them up for tea, thinking they might melt and make nice sweeteners for the steaming brew. Who knew? She wasn't posh. She wasn't cultured. She liked her sweet tooth, and if the candy didn't dissolve she'd still have a treat when she reached the bottom of her china cup.

However, how was she to know that the assorted soft candies left on her doorstep the night before were not from a secret admirer but rather the abandoned children of a lost traveler among the stars? That the traveler's race, though tiny, was deadly when crossed and not prone to forgiving transgressions? So when Karen unsealed the little plastic package of rainbow-colored gummies, she simply released them from their airlocked space. That was no matter; they were adaptable. But they could not, apparently, adapt to scalding liquid.

So as Karen poured the freshly brewed tea into her clean, white china cup, she was ill-prepared for the screams of agony emitted by the little orange gummy resting in its bottom. She gasped and nearly dropped the pot. Then chastising herself for her foolishness, she realized there must have been an air-pocket or something in the candy that caused the squealing noise. Oh well, it'd still taste fine.

She popped the little orange gummy, now flattened and mushy, onto her waiting tongue, bit down, and swallowed. The squealing stopped.

But Orangie's brothers and sisters started, and soon she lay bleeding on the floor from a thousand small bites. They were insanely fast. As she watched the rainbow assortment of gummies advance on her prone figure, she realized that Orangie was the lucky one.

He had been consumed in a single bite.

The Price

Raquel and Thom had been married for over fifty years before their transfers took place. After a lifetime together, they transitioned to their new bodies on the New Eden colony without complication. Their brains, the only parts of their bodies that were truly irreplaceable, experienced rejuvenation from chemical saturation as if they had been born again. In a way, they had.

Had enough of Planet Earth? Nothing left to keep you here? Become a colonist, and live the life you've always dreamed…

Raquel ran to Thom, taking great, striding leaps in New Eden's low gravity. He laughed as she tumbled into his arms, kissing him fiercely. "Hey," he said, once his mouth was free again, "what's gotten into you?"

"You, hopefully," she said, winking. "I want to test this new body out and see if we're getting our money's worth." She moved close, her breasts pressed against his chest, and reached down with one slender hand. "So far, everything seems to be functioning at full capacity." She grinned.

You'll have your choice of several new worlds to explore…

It was no wonder. The beauty of her eighteen-year old womanhood enchanted him every bit as much as her human body had, so many years ago. The Corporation certainly had done its job well, and he could only hope she would be equally satisfied with his own renewal. Even if they offered money-back guarantees, how could anybody compete with fifty years of companionship? Whatever form she was preserved in, as long as her mind was there, he was happy.

And you'll discover a whole new lease on life!

The solution in every android's head cavity nurtured

the human brain housed within its walls—cushioned by soft membranes, yet protected by the nearly indestructible artificial body. Sensors placed throughout the synthetic epidermis mimicked the sensation of human skin. Electronic eyes and ears relayed information to the biological components of the brain.

A variety of affordable payment plans are available for your financial needs.

As Thom held Raquel's new body, he felt every bit as close to her as he had when she had been young and fully human. The eyes that looked into his own mirrored the ones he'd fallen in love with fifty years ago. The lips he kissed gave the same gentle resistance he'd remembered. Was it too much to hope for another fifty years?

You'll see things from an entirely different perspective!

Housed within her synthetic body, Jenn felt the press of the man she'd desired for as long as she could remember. Bribing the surgeon to dispose of her sister's brain and substitute her own had cost her life savings; but this was the opportunity of a lifetime.

After all, wasn't love worth the price?

No Man's Land

Through her mind, plots ran like wild dogs she chased but never caught. They outran her, and now, finally, she didn't even have strength for the chase anymore. She watched the scenes play out in fragments in her head, shattered images like reflections from a broken mirror.

She wondered why she had bothered to try for so long. She remembered Emily Dickinson's drawer full of poetry, found after her death, and laughed bitterly. At least poor Emily lived on in a way through the people that came after her. She had no such luxury.

In the short time she had left, she lost herself in illusion, escaping the loneliness by losing herself in happy times that never were. She bent over the tattered, torn papers of her earlier efforts. She wondered how much longer her light would last before… She read and plunged into her self-created fantasy world.

The pristine condition of the find amazed him, especially the positioning of the manuscript so close to the bones of the hand. He scraped away more dirt with a small brush, mindful of the ancient relics.

Soon he was joined by another anthropologist, a colleague who had noticed his hunched profile. Neither trill nor warble passed between the two. They exchanged a look that spoke volumes and bent to the task of unearthing the ancient human treasure.

With the help of others, they would catalog and number the finds for the museum. The site's discovery promised to be a major contribution to the field. The wrecked buildings, the warped metal beams, the skeletal remains and parchments. Destruction of the seemingly permanent next to fragile remains of flesh and trees that had survived a billion years. Perhaps, hidden in the manuscript, they'd finally find the key to the catastrophe that wiped out the human species.

Bread

The mother and son contemplated the overturned bread truck with mixed emotions. Though they hadn't eaten for days, the interior of the innocent looking white vehicle might hold more than they wished to see. Josie told her son to hide nearby while she investigated. The doors must have fallen shut after the truck was looted, because the inside was empty of almost everything save some debris and the slowly transforming corpse in the driver's seat. Josie, driven by morbid curiosity, leaned forward to gaze upon all that remained of the unfortunate soul.

Fungal growth transformed his skin bizarre shades of yellow and green like some horrific chia pet, while long velvety shoots grew from his eyes, nose, and ears, permanently fixing him to his seat.

She knew she should hurry before other scavengers returned, but simple human decency prevented her. She wanted to close his eyes.

Leaning over the driver, she broke off the eye stalks. Weird tendrils reached out for her like spectral hands. She batted them away, loosing more spores into the air like a fine mist.

She tried to shield her mouth and coughed, sharp loud exhalations racking her body.

"Mommy?"

She closed the lids, a futile gesture since their thin skin would soon sprout more alien tendrils. As she turned back to address her son, she spotted, out of the corner of her eye, the clear plastic of a loaf of bread wedged between driver and door. She made to grab it when her son called again.

"Mommy! Someone's coming!"

Noticing the mold inside the wrapping, she threw the loaf aside in disgust. They hadn't eaten in days but were not yet desperate enough to stomach such fare, even given their supposed immunity to the spores' malignant effects. They might not lose their minds to the alien fungus, but simple food poisoning could kill them just as well. She ran out to her son.

None too soon, she reached Jack and ducked behind a large piece of concrete debris—carnage from the past weeks' mayhem. They peered over its edge at the walking dead, descending upon the bread truck as if they needed the food. But of course, they did. Their masters beckoned, and they would not stop until the Earth was picked clean and seeded with their monstrous spores.

Finding nothing, they exited and walked, single file, in the direction of the mother-ship. Josie hugged her son, remembering similar lines for bread and unemployment only weeks before, lines they might have shared with those same unfortunates. She knew that she and her son would never walk such a line again.

At least their deaths would be clean. She wiped the green spores from her clothes, grabbed Jack's hand, and ran into the shadows.

What Might Have Been

When she saw the small jello pyramid, she knew she'd waited much too long to clean the fridge. Tiny green creatures bowed before the surprisingly rigid structure, prostrate with piety.

Then they spotted her.

The descendants of some particularly nasty leftovers screamed in terror at the sight of her. Well, some of them did. Others cowered behind either the lime-colored pyramid or an open box of baking soda. Many ran to a tinfoil monstrosity covered by mold spores, but for all she knew it might have been their nursery. Still others gathered weapons to defend themselves against the coming onslaught. Their wise men (wise molds?) had prophesied of the time of the coming of the great blue bottle, unleashing its deadly spray, and the monster who would one day wield it.

They stole toothpicks from ancient leftovers and waved them at her.

Sally sighed and sprayed the cleaner, wiping out the beginnings of a promising new civilization. She really needed to clean the damn fridge more often.

Cat Russell

Paperweight

The small bit of pink seemed to float amid the frozen bubbles as the girl held the clear, translucent globe in her hand. "What is it?" she asked. "It's lovely."

"Oh, it's a paperweight," said the gent behind the counter. He leaned back in the antique swivel rocker and stared at ceiling tiles. A fire burned lazily in the old fashioned fireplace of the shop.

"No, I mean…obviously it's a paperweight, but what *is* it?" she said, pointing to the rosy pastel branches inside the glass.

"What? Oh…oh, that. That's coral." His mouth twitched slightly. He adjusted the spectacles perched on his reddened nose.

"Coral?" Carrie asked again. Stray wisps of long brown hair fell in front of her eyes as she held the globe closer to her face. She enjoyed the cool feel of it cradled in her hands. "What's it for?"

"For?" asked the old man, perking up. "I don't know that it's 'for' anything, young lady."

Carrie hated when old people called her 'young lady.' She found it condescending.

The shop owner continued, "Coral is a living thing, you know. Not this one, obviously; it's just a skeleton…of a creature that used to live in the water."

Her mind immediately went to the frozen lake. She'd never seen such creatures there before, but she could snorkel for them once the ice broke. "Where do they live? I mean…do they hide under rocks or leaves or something in the water?"

The old man pushed the glasses up his bulbous nose again, threw his head back, and laughed.

Carrie felt stupid. What was his problem?

Snorting a little, the old man took a dirty rag from

his shirt pocket and wiped his eyes beneath the lenses. "Oh…Pardon me, Miss! I didn't mean…no." He sobered up. "No, my dear, corals are…um, were huge." He looked up again, this time at a past she couldn't see. "Coral reefs spanned miles and miles in the Atlantic." He took in her irritated, puzzled expression. "No, my dear," he said, "you're right. It's not funny." He gathered his thoughts a moment before adding, "It's rather sad really. No more coral reefs." He continued staring into the distance. "And no Atlantic Ocean either. At least," he added, "not for you."

"I don't understand," the girl said. *Atlantic? Ocean? Was this guy crazy?*

"Well, the Atlantic was one of several oceans on Earth. They were huge, spread out over the whole planet. They were so huge they never completely froze. Can you imagine that? There were miles and miles of warm salt water just filled with life. Fish, mammals, and other wonders. The seas were full of color and mystery."

Listening to the old man, Carrie looked again at the fragment of color in her hand. From his description, she could almost smell the sharp tang of an ocean filled with a riot of color and life.

The winter wind blew through a chink in the door, snapping her from her reverie. The old man seemed to snap back to the present too. He pulled his heavy coat more closely around him before continuing.

"But that was a long time ago," he said. "Before pollution killed the corals and most of the fish died." He looked at her with large, watery eyes. "All that's left now is sad little remnants of the past." He nodded at the sphere. "Like the one you hold in your hands."

She looked at him, shocked.

"Are you saying this is an actual 'Earth Relic?'" She could barely get the words out.

The old man nodded. "Go on, my dear. Take it. I'm afraid it's about all my generation can give today's youth. That and stories."

Carrie cradled the glass orb in her gloved hands, nodded to the old man, and left. The bell made a pleasant tinkling noise as the wooden door shut behind her. She realized the old man was living history, just as the coral she held was a piece of history too. They both told stories of the past, and she, for one, was ready to listen.

FANTASY

Cat Russell

The Tree of Good and Evil

Blood thundered in my ears as I entered the darkened, dusty atmosphere of the bookstore. The building attracted me: brick walls of burnt sienna, an aged mustard-colored door that squeaked as I pulled on the brass handle, the rooms inside lined by mountains of books piled haphazardly down every aisle. Literary avalanches spilled from overflowing shelves of deep brown wood. Inside, amber light illuminated everything. It smelled of yellowed parchment, dust mites, and possibility. How could I resist?

The proprietor sat behind a mahogany counter. His stare unnerved me, and I quickly turned a corner, out of his sight but yet still felt his eyes on me. However, I would not let that deter me from what promised to be an exciting expedition. Lately, so many independent bookstores had been replaced, driven out of business by cookie cutter enterprises with glitzy cafes, harsh lighting, and immaculate untouched books. This store was my palate cleanser, a visit into the past—into a time when bookstores had individual personalities and bibliophiles could discover unexpected delights hidden among the stacks. Even if the cashier gave me chills. A slight shiver ran down my spine as I strode deeper into his domain.

I wandered the maze of shelving and paperback aisles to find myself dead-ended in a dark corner marked "Religion/Mythology." A Bible with pages of gold-leaf caught my eye. The cover, in letters of faded gilt, read King James Version: Annotated historical edition, Samael Arcangeli editor. My own strict religious adherence had fallen by the wayside years ago, but this title intrigued me. Historical edition? Edited by Samael? It was a joke, and a tasteless one at that—considering it was mocking one of the most sacred texts in history. The book seemed the type of special edition favored by presses that released Jane Austen books with zombies: mass entertainment masked as cultural humor. I held the heavy tome, felt the weight of years, and sniffed the pages; it smelled like history.

Upon closer inspection, I discovered the book had

been wedged between Joseph Campbell's *Hero's Journey* and *Edith Hamilton's Mythology*. Wondering how deliberate the placement was, I grabbed the other two books as well before taking my purchases to face the cryptic clerk in the front once more.

His coal black eyes sparked at my approach. He said, "So, you're a history enthusiast, I see."

I hesitated before replying. For a moment, I wasn't sure he was joking. I said, "Obviously not."

"Ahhh," he continued with an appreciative grin, "This…This is one of my favorites." He brandished the heavy Bible at me like a sword, one handed—as though it was light as an angel's feather.

I asked, "You've read it?"

He chuckled, the sound resonating deep in his chest. "Read it? You could say that." He looked me up and down. "I wrote—well, edited it."

He had to be kidding. The book was obviously a relic. At first I thought it a mere marketing trick, but no, the creak of the stiffened cover bending, the sound of ancient pages turning like the pull of ocean waves beneath the full moon, the weirdly luminescent letters signaled both age and the promise of something new. But this was not new. This was something very, very old.

After another moment, I broke into an uncertain grin. Was he a fellow humanist, such as myself? "I've always enjoyed the classics." Then thinking he might yet offer some genuine information about my purchase, I asked, "Seriously, what's up with this? It's a pretty unconventional edition, considering it's so old. Do you know anything about it?"

Placing the book carefully on the counter, on top of the other two, he answered. "Seriously? Of course, I'm serious. This book is about as truthful as these other two,"—he tapped the two mythology books—"but lacked the necessary editorial notes to give readers perspective." He pulled a faded receipt book from an unseen drawer and scrawled in it. "I'd be interested to hear what you think. Most people's eyes scan right over it. Interesting how yours were drawn straight to it."

Wind roared in my ears. I felt as though I were on the edge of some great precipice, my choice clear before me: either return to the safety of my previous position or step into the unknown. I breathed deeply: in through my nose, out through my mouth. The exercise calmed me.

"Yes," I said. Taking another step I added, "I thought the choice to lump the religious section with the mythology one was a bit daring, considering today's climate of political correctness."

"You know that's not what this is."

His eyes unnerved me. I felt as though the two of us were alone in the whole world, and he offered forbidden fruit.

"In a way, that's correct," he said, answering my unspoken thought. "Knowledge has always been the fruit forbidden by a certain someone, hasn't it? Just look at what happened to poor Prometheus." He winked and leaned forward. "I'm assuming you are familiar with his story, given your purchases today." He tapped the mythology book.

"He stole fire from the gods to give to mankind." I couldn't help myself. I felt compelled to speak.

"Yes, he did. He felt sorry for mankind, forced to live in the dark and the cold, because Zeus wanted to keep fire in the heavens. He paid a heavy price for his generosity."

"The vulture, I know. It would come to feed on him daily, but being an immortal, he couldn't die." The air seemed heavier. "He would heal to be tormented again the next day," I added, and saw sorrow in his eyes.

"It's just another version of the fruit in the garden. Both times, the supreme deity wanted to keep the light of knowledge for himself, keep his creatures ignorant to better rule them, horribly punish an immortal for the temerity of sharing knowledge with mankind."

"So you're saying God's a tyrant?" I asked, with a nervous little laugh. I couldn't help but feel he knew these stories too well.

"I'm saying Prometheus was a hero…or the serpent, whatever you want to call me. They change my name in every story, but the message is the same."

Ah, so that was his angle, I told myself, though I shuddered when he handed me the red-inked receipt. I had always thought of myself as a spiritual person and this talk made me uncomfortable. Yet I couldn't seem to stop, felt the authenticity of his words. "Why do you come off so badly then…in the Bible?"

"Consider the source." His dark eyes bore into me once more.

"God?"

He snorted, then laughed full and loud. "Hell, no. Mankind. It's written throughout the ages by different authors and finally compiled into this collection of stories that bear some resemblance to truth but…well, have you ever played 'Operator?'"

"Of course."

"Imagine a game of 'Operator' that spanned not a room over minutes but eons and numerous peoples. Is it any wonder the stories are garbled? The same goes for the myths of almost every culture. I'm the trickster, the tempter, the sorter of good from evil. I'm free will versus servitude, the rebel versus the dictator. I'm Chaos Incarnate, as opposed to Order Imposed. Hell, just look at my store!"

Like an idiot, I actually turned and looked around. Books in piles everywhere, every shelf, every nook and cranny filled to the brim and beyond with books of every subject. "The bookstore?" I said.

"Look at my track record versus his, and I'm only directly referencing two mythologies now since I know you aren't familiar with them all. But 'pagan' mythos saw the serpent as a symbol of knowledge for a reason. God reinforces ignorance, calls for faith instead of reason, forbids knowledge and the betterment of mankind. I advocate educating yourselves."

As a product of the Twentieth century, I agreed with the sentiment despite years of religious upbringing. True, I had forsaken mass and the confessional long ago, but not spirituality. The lessons of our youth stay with us throughout our lives. I had been brought up to see the devil as the villain in the saga of the heavens, but Lucifer meant "Light Bringer," the most beautiful of angels before he fell. Prometheus meant forethought, an indication of the beauty of his mind. Even serpents reflected the myriad colors of the rainbow. Could I have believed for so long the hero to be a villain, simply because he was not allowed to tell his own story? He lost his voice when he lost his cause.

He handed me the books and the handwritten receipt. Thinking there had been some mistake, I handed him my card, but he shook his head and wouldn't take it. "I don't need anything from you," he said. "I told you I wanted to educate the world. What better way is there than through books?"

I started to protest, how would he stay in business?—but knew before the words left my mouth that they were useless. I took my divine gifts, and as I left the store, looked down at the red-inked receipt. In ancient scrawling script, it said, "Thank you. And please, come back again."

As the door closed behind me, I knew I had found what I needed.

Reclamation

The doe entered the church without fear. The enormous oaken doors had been propped open just enough to let her in—almost as if the god of this house expected her, and the echo of her steps accompanied her inside the garish edifice. This was not her idea of holy ground. The gold that glittered on the marble altar paled compared to the sunlight dappling the floor of her forest home. What god could reside in such a cold, barren place?

He walked out to greet her, a host welcoming an honored guest, but to her he was the invader claiming her ancestral lands as his own. She had tolerated his presence while distracted with human encroachment upon her lands, but no more—humanity had pushed her world to the brink of annihilation. She now realized the two were tied together, as the tangled boughs of a tree in a storm were inextricably linked. She needed to break those limbs to rid herself of both: the two-legged had brought the god along with them, and his protection emboldened their further destruction of her domain.

She viewed the mockery above the altar, the torn and molded skeleton of her forest sister made to support the outstretched bloody arms of this dying god. He was but a child to her, ancient as she was, and despite her slight and gentle appearance, her rage embodied all the power and force of the winter's storm, the crashing currents of the river, the power of growing things to break apart the immovable, the unmalleable, the static. All knew how a slight crack, filled by rainwater, would freeze and break the strongest of boulders. She would teach him the ways of the old gods, and he would flee or perish again—a final time, never to return.

Her eyes burned with golden light as the crucifix grew behind the walking god. He turned to see new shoots spring from the dead wood, her forest sister killed to prop his worship. She too knew how to bring back the dead. Tendrils shot from both the bottom and sides of the cross, the horizontal shoots reaching to tear the human image from its nut-brown body, hurling it at the startled deity with all the force it could muster. The cathedral was filled with deafening groans, as every forest creature forced by human hands to honor this dying god reclaimed their original forms. Wooden altars grew roots, tearing up the marble floors. The beams supporting the vaulted ceiling sprouted limbs, emerald green leaves growing alongside wooden arms that burst through the stained glass dome, letting in the blessed natural sunlight. Their beams fell on the younger god's crown, the thorns growing deeper into his soft flesh until he fled from his adopted home, his temple of human ingenuity.

The doe herself grew to fill the space, walking to what had once been the altar, to sit upon her wooden throne.

Password

Saint Peter scanned the Book of Life and frowned. "Sorry, but you're not listed."

The woman paled. "You mean…?"

Peter's frown deepened. He scratched his white robe, adjusted his halo. "Sorry, but I can't admit you."

"But I went to church, volunteered—"

"Are you suggesting God made a clerical error?"

"Well, not God personally, no, but somewhere along the bureaucracy—"

"I'll see what I can do." From his robe, he pulled a PDA and tapped the screen. "I'll put in your…yee-es. Seems there's been a major snafu concerning your demise, sorry. Your override password is being emailed to you."

From the woman's coat, a sharp ping sounded. She pulled out a dripping cell phone. "It still works?"

Saint Peter fixed her with his steely gaze. "You drowned and your consciousness still functions, so why wouldn't your phone work?"

She shook water from the cell. "Dammit…uh, *darn*. I can't remember how to sign in. Must be the trauma of death and all."

Peter shook his head. "Sorry, but if you aren't on the list, then the Pearly Gates only open by the override password sent you in that email. I can't access it. It's personal."

"Is this some test? Like a riddle? I mean, the gates aren't pearly. They're silver and gold."

Saint Peter patted her in friendly condescension. "It's a misnomer. Tell you what, I'll see what I can do on this end, and in the meantime find a nice place to haunt." He placed the PDA somewhere in the folds of his robe, then added, "I hear Jamaica's nice this time of year."

Hell of a Job

"Let's go in here for a drink," Elsa said, pointing at the bright neon sign. 'Brimstone Corner' blinked off and on against the night.

I followed her in, eager to drown my sorrows. She walked to the bar and ordered two Shirley Temples. Who the hell orders Shirley Temples in a bar, for Chris'sake? With one smooth motion the bartender set two bright pink concoctions on the counter before us. "On the house," he said. He didn't crack a smile. Nothing. In fact, I bet if he said anything else, his face would have cracked like ice dropped in a cauldron.

"Come on, Sharon, drink up!" she chided as I stared at the sickly pink liquid. "You were the best damned waitress they had. They were fools to let you go!"

"And after I took so much of their crap too," I sulked. "I can't believe I wore that stupid housfrau uniform either."

Elsa smiled. "Too good for them, that's what you are," she said, then nodded to the drink in my hand. "Go ahead. Drink up!"

"No thanks," I said, setting it down. "I'm not really thirsty, after all."

"Suit yourself," she said, shrugged, and sipped her drink.

I took a look around. A guy dressed like Genghis Khan sat playing cards with a man in a suit and fedora. At another table, a Caesar wannabe read a newspaper while some guy dressed like a Nazi drank tea from a mug. An open area near the karaoke machine served as a makeshift stage for two slinky women in devil costumes singing 'Copa Cabana' off key. I mean, *way* off key.

I turned to the barman. A sticker on his shirt pocket

said 'My name is' with 'Bub' printed neatly underneath in black marker. "Uh, sir?" I said. I did *not* want to call this guy 'Bub' even if it was his name. He seemed offended by the moon shining in the window; it illuminated the floating dust and cigar smoke hanging in the air. "Sir?" I said again.

He said nothing. Just stared.

I looked around for a sign or something. Nothing. I looked for Elsa, but she had wandered off to join the two succubi in a chorus of 'Day-O.' Curiosity was killing me so I decided to risk the man's facial fracture for an answer. "What's tonight? Is it some sort of Halloween party or something?" Dumb question maybe, but it was July.

"I hear you're a good waitress," he said.

"Ummm, thanks," I responded, taken by surprise. "But as I was saying…"

"We could use a good waitress around here," Bub continued, not paying attention to my question.

"Okay, but I wanted to know…wait, huh?" The place was a dive, but really, I couldn't be too picky in this economy.

Bub stared off into the distance. The sound of a demonic chorus of 'Making Love Out of Nothing at All' faded into the background. "Yeah, we've needed some help ever since our last waiter had…an unfortunate accident."

"What kind of accident?" I didn't like the sound of that.

"The kind where he couldn't work here anymore."

"Oh, well, uh…okay." Maybe he was on Workman's Comp. I eyed the barman suspiciously. He didn't seem the violent type, just moody, but he was pretty damn big just the same.

He wiped the counter absentmindedly and watched the karaoke some more. The women were apparently arguing over which selection they'd butcher next. Elsa gesticulated wildly towards the machine to illustrate her point. After a moment, he continued, "I couldn't pay you in money, but you don't really need it here anyway. I'd provide your food and drink, and you'd get a small apartment overhead."

Shocked, I asked, "Seriously? No money?" I had quite a few debts.

"No," he said, picking up a glass and wiping the jar. "But like I said, there are other compensations. Besides not having to worry about the necessities of life," he chuckled softly before continuing. "Besides *that*, we're a pretty diverse crowd." He gestured to the tables spread throughout the room. "There's really no code here for you to worry about. I couldn't care less how you conduct your affairs, as long as you do your job and serve the patrons."

"Do I get to keep my tips, at least?"

"You won't be getting any tips."

Disbelief clouded my features. I whispered to him, "Listen, even if the customers are cheap, every once in a while I'm sure I'll get a tip. Couldn't I keep that?"

"No," he said, setting the glass under the counter. He brought his face inches away from mine. "You don't understand. You don't get paid. Sure, the place isn't fancy, but there are other perks." He grinned. "You get to live, for one thing."

I backed up, right into Elsa. She'd given up singing to come check on me. "You explain everything to her yet, Bub?"

"I don't understand… What?" I turned wildly between the barman and the woman I'd thought was my friend. I looked around again. Demons singing Calypso music. Nazis, Roman Emperors, and Mafioso sat drinking and playing cards.

"I told you," said Bub slowly, as if speaking to a child. "You get to live. Well, you get an afterlife anyway." He laughed maniacally. I never believed anyone truly laughed like that before, but he sounded like some evil, menacing cartoon villain.

Elsa cackled gleefully behind me. "Don't you get it?" she said. "It's this or oblivion. Which is it going to be?" She pushed my Shirley Temple closer to me. "If you want the job, all you've got to do is take a drink."

I looked around. It was obvious, really. Hell, I should have known the moment I stepped in there. The karaoke alone gave it away.

"I'll take the job," I said and swigged my drink. After all, I thought as I gazed around the bar, at least there wasn't a dress code.

The Game

Cara gripped the polyhedral dice in her hands with all the force she could muster. If she had enough strength, she'd crush the small hard shapes into powder. But she didn't, so all that happened was the quick, dull throbbing where the sharp corners bit into the soft flesh of her palm. The game had been especially grueling. But they were an elite group, the best of the best, and the DM had offered an incentive to the last soul standing too precious to resist. One by one, the members of their party died, until she alone remained—along with her nemesis across the table.

"Come on, roll already," called the pimply youth, his greasy raven hair not quite covering his black rimmed eyes. Moisture trickled down his scalp. His body odor reminded Cara of rock concerts: the smell of sweat, stale beer, and vomit.

She half threw, half dropped the dice, then watched the small crimson shape travel a short distance across the table before stopping. The numeral twenty sat on top, like an accusation.

"Shit!" cried her tormentor. "What the fuck did you do that for?"

She said nothing, her only answer the glare she shot him. If looks could kill, his corpse would long ago have been bleeding meat left to rot on the floor.

"Okay," said the DM. "Your spell binds Andrew, enslaves his mind, and forces him to your will. What do you do?"

A slow smile spread across her face, like liquid fire. Andrew's already milk-white skin blanched.

"I trap him inside these dice." She picked up her D20 and eyed it closely.

"Wouldn't you rather use him for something

practical?" The DM glanced at the now blubbering man.

"No. It amuses me to have him *literally* in the palm of my hand."

Andrew backed away, but the DM nodded, and Cara held the blood red dice toward her victim. Dark lines like veins ran through them, pulsing like the hearts of its previous victims, its newest victim.

"Besides, what would he be useful for? He's a waste of space."

Andrew viewed his own hands with horror as his skin began fading, tearing itself from his bones, hurling itself toward the contents of Cara's hand. Muscles and cartilage followed. His blood steamed, joining the spiral of death like a fine red mist. His screams cut short when his throat ripped away, then finally the stripped bones disintegrated, the fine white powder twisting toward the deepening crimson die, til nothing remained of what had moments before been an arrogant, asinine prick.

The Demon Master nodded his approval. The Dark Arts were not for the faint of heart and tended to attract two kinds of people: bullies bent on subjugating others to feed their own lust for dominance, and the bullied who hit their limit long before and wanted revenge. It didn't matter to him which of them won the game; his kingdom benefited from both types of souls in the end. Sometimes, happily, they even overlapped.

He gazed at his champion with approval. Demonic RPG's were not for the faint of heart, and modern practitioners of Dark Magic had much to gain from indulging in his little pastime. He didn't mind granting some powerful magical abilities for a laughably short human lifetime. What did eighty, ninety, even one hundred short mortal years matter when he'd gain their souls for eternity?

But he enjoyed it when the bullied won. Underdogs had a special place in what passed for his heart.

The Last Time

The sweet aroma hung heavy in the air as the creature watched the young girl collect flowers. Roses, violets, and daffodils lined the path she strode, but the strongest scent by far was jasmine.

The girl's loveliness exceeded that of the garden. Her hair flowed down her back like a cascade of shimmering gold. Milky white skin, rosebud lips, and sea green eyes attracted the demon to her. The bushes rustled slightly as the fiend leaned closer, mouth open, fangs exposed.

"Who's there?" called the girl. She dropped more flowers into the basket and turned toward the sound. No one answered.

The demon returned to his realm. Overcome by the shadowy reflection of the heaven he'd left behind, the banished angel clutched one thin jasmine strand. His punishment had not rid him of the desire for love and beauty, only the ability to experience it. Hot tears stung his cheeks, even as the flower in his hand withered, filling the air with the smell of burning jasmine.

Cat Russell

Mirror

Sebastian had heard family stories about the relic in the attic for years. However, even as a curious child he had always been sensible and never believed the rumors of what lay beyond the locked door. Spirits and ghosts had no place in his imagination.

Nevertheless, the large standing object covered by the thin azure sheet had been gathering dust in a disused recess of the attic for centuries, according to family legend. The grandparents of his grandparents had feared the item hidden beneath the heavenly blue, yet feared to let it go; the consequences of its guardianship falling into careless hands might be too great.

In all likelihood, his elders had created the stories to keep meddlesome children from scavenging through old family heirlooms, though Sebastian discovered nothing else of interest except a few scraps of antique clothing and some worn furniture. The secret hidden beneath the sheet would be revealed as nothing more than an ordinary mirror from a garage sale. With luck though, it might be valuable as an antique.

He pulled the silk off in one smooth motion, coughing from the dust born on the air like dandelion seeds. The cloud dispersed, and he gazed at the image of the mirrored-attic. The same wooden walls, crossbeams, old trunks, and debris of generations reflected back in reverse. But the staring face was not his own. The features were similar, high cheekbones, large round eyes and full sensual lips, but there any resemblance ended. Its deep brown eyes stared back at him from within a pale, hairless face. It lifted thin, bare hands to cover its mouth before it ran, screaming from the room.

Sebastian himself stepped back, reeling from the shock, grabbing at his face, his head, his horns. He sighed in relief when he felt his tail swish around his shoulders. He was fine. Who *was* that then—some demonic version of himself trapped in a mirror world? He wondered if the beast was dangerous. Should he destroy the cursed mirror and rid himself of whatever lurked inside?

In the corner of the mirror, the blue cover was barely visible near the doorway of the looking-glass room. The creature returned to stand before him, and Sebastian took a step back. Then, overcome with pity for the poor bald thing trapped on the other side, Sebastian placed a lone claw upon the glass. The monster's eyes widened in terror, and it struck the translucent partition with something long and hard.

The mirror shattered.

Sebastian's last thoughts cut as deeply as the shards of falling crystal. He felt himself break into a thousand pieces.

The man's sigh filled the room.

Grabbing a broom, he hastily swept the fragments of broken glass onto the discarded sheet, then wrapped them tightly in their sky-colored shroud and entombed them in the waste bin. He shoved the bin away with his foot, once more sending clouds of dust into the attic's stale air. Turning his back on all, he hastily closed the door and locked it behind him.

Later he could tell himself it had only been a dream.

Cat Russell

Ghost Writer

Ethan's first shock was waking up in a coffin. His second was realizing that it wasn't a prank played by fellow carousers after another night's drinking binge. He gazed upon the proof; his parents sat amid other black-clad mourners—his friends, coworkers, his estranged sister, and a pastor in a tweed suit.

He felt his jaw drop, but when he looked down at his body it was still closed. Strange that he should feel the same without a body. He strained to remember the details of his death. No bruises appeared on his face or hands, but then he remembered his sister, Alicia, telling him that funeral parlors employed makeup artists. That was probably why.

He sat on the coffin's lip and watched the crowd. How depressing. His parents were upset, and the only "friends" that showed up were drinking buddies and a couple dry-eyed people from the office…probably so they could get the day off. He had no wife, no children, and now that he had all the time in the world, he realized he'd never really lived.

Crap.

Why was he still here?

He remembered some movie, years ago, said ghosts needed to complete "unfinished business." Something to do with taking care of things they should have done during their lives. There must be something he needed to do.

He knew what it had to be, but he was still a bloody coward, even dead. However, necessity pushed him forward.

He needed to find a psychic. Luckily, he had seen a sign for one shortly before his untimely demise.

Zelda the Magnificent had chosen her name with care. She called herself 'Zelda' after F. Scott Fitzgerald's wife, and she felt the aura that came with the name fit her profession rather well. Closing her eyes, she let her fingers hover over the glowing crystal ball. A small blue-haired octogenarian peered into the orb.

The globe's light burned more brightly as Zelda pressed her foot farther down on the pedal beneath the table.

"Well?" said the old woman.

"Hush," said Madam Zelda, flooring the cold blue steel. "The dead come and go as they will. They feel no more the rush of mortal life."

"But I'm paying by the hour!" complained Zelda's only paying customer.

"Your husband will come soon. I feel it," said Zelda.

"Don't forget to ask him about the insurance policy!" said the woman.

All the lights extinguished, even the ball, plunging the room into darkness. A luminous, ghostly form stood behind the old woman.

"Who the hell are you?" asked Zelda.

After Zelda's client had been told their session would reconvene at a later time (for a small fee), Madam Z returned to her workplace, switched on the lights, and demanded an explanation.

Ethan didn't know where to begin. After a few minutes of confused stuttering, he blurted, "But you're a psychic!"

"No, that's just what I tell my clients," said Zelda, taking off her wig and lighting a cigarette. "Now, what I want to know is what the hell you're up to. You can't seriously think I'm going to fall for your ghost trick." She made scare quotes in the air around the words. A cigarette danced loosely in the corner of her mouth as she spoke.

Ethan walked through the table to prove his point.

"Holographic projector," said Madam Zelda.

"What do you think this is? Star Trek?" asked Ethan.

"I don't know. You supposed to be an alien or something?"

"I'm a ghost. I'd think that'd be obvious to a psychic."

"Try again, Sunshine."

Ethan concentrated and, with considerable effort, pushed coins around the table.

"Magnets."

"It's your table."

"So?"

After repeated tests of his veracity, Zelda finally conceded Ethan was telling the truth. She leaned back in her chair, sipped a mint julep, and let Ethan unfold his plans to her.

"So, all I need to do is break in, do your dirty work, and I get a cut of the profits?" she said.

Ethan nodded with enthusiasm.

"I'm in."

An hour later, Zelda's clunker was parked behind Ethan's former residence. After the ghost had checked everything out, he gave her a thumbs up, and she walked to the back door. The key was under the mat, just like he said. With security like that, it's a wonder he lived as long as he did, she thought.

Once inside, she scanned the cramped house for the object of their desire. Ethan hovered over the desk in the corner. Apparently, his parents hadn't cleaned everything out yet. Too soon after the funeral, probably still trying to make sense of it all, blah blah blah. All she cared about was getting the job done so she could make a profit and they could both depart.

"It's in here?" she asked.

Ethan nodded.

She pulled open the drawer. It was unlocked. The papers were there, just as he'd promised. She slid them into the envelope she'd brought, then took out another paper and a pen.

Licking the envelope closed, she stuck several stamps along the top edge, and walked outside. Ethan followed her closely. She walked to the corner. "Now, you do your part, as promised."

Ethan took the pen, concentrated, concentrated some more, and painstakingly scrawled his signature along the bottom line.

"Ready?" she asked, holding the envelope before the mailbox. Ethan waited a moment, then nodded again. She dropped it inside. "There," she said. "You've submitted your manuscript to a publisher. If accepted, I'll be left the profits. If not, you still submitted your work. Your business is finished." She smiled. "You can move on now."

Ethan grinned. Then the ground opened beneath his feet, and he plummeted. The portal closed, leaving behind only a small whiff of smoke and the smell of sulphur.

Zelda wiped her hands on her pants and sighed. "They never think that far ahead," she said to no one in particular. Then she turned once more to the house to retrieve any valuables before the parents showed up.

Cat Russell

The Ring

The house fire took everything Cynthia cared about, including her life. The only copy of her manuscript, which she had typed on an old fashioned typewriter in a fit of romantic sentimentality, had been incinerated. Her body, which she had taken such pride in keeping healthy and strong, had been reduced to ash when the home she had known for the past four years had burned to the ground. Her only companion had been her tabby, Gertrude, but rather than warn her owner of the inferno, she had done the sensible feline thing and saved her own ass. Cynthia didn't blame her.

Hindsight is twenty-twenty, and that goes double when you're a ghost. Sure, trauma had driven her to a life of seclusion, but present circumstances made her rethink the decisions she had made. If she had lived closer to town, maybe a neighbor would have seen the fire. As things stood, the firefighters only happened on her home because of the forest blaze. Now, her consciousness didn't even have a body, dead or alive, to cling to. The only thing left was the ring she had been wearing when she died.

Her spirit had condensed and become contained within that tiny metal band when she had shuffled off her mortal coil.

Most of the firefighters had walked farther off, but two remained close to her former home. From within the ring's shining band, Cynthia watched one of them approach. "Hey, Bill," said the female firefighter, picking the ring up to show her companion. "Hear anything about family, next of kin?"

"Nah, sweetheart," said Bill. The condescending endearment made the firewoman wince while Cynthia psychically winced on her behalf. Cynthia *knew* that voice; even through the grime and the distortion of the ring, she'd recognize that face anywhere. Though dead, her first impulse was to run away, her second—to warn the woman.

How could she forget that monster? Four years ago, he

had turned her world upside down. He had said he'd find her again, that she belonged to him body and soul, but she had moved! Changed her name, secluded herself and dear God, how did he find her?

Hiding had done her no good. Now was the time for action. Before he hurt someone else.

"Nobody that I know of," he continued, oblivious to both women's distress, "but you could find out when we get back to the station."

"Thanks, Bill," said the woman, whose name Cynthia learned was "Eve" from the lettering on her fluorescent yellow jacket. Eve examined the ring a moment longer before slipping it into her pocket. Instinctually, Cynthia prodded, mentally probing the woman's psyche. Seeming to reconsider, Eve put the ring on her finger instead.

Immediately, Cynthia felt the rush of life in her new body, the woman's strength, the ache of her muscles, the warmth of her browned skin. She even smelled the ash in the air. Was she breathing in her old body from within her new one? Eve's body turned to gaze at her coworker through new eyes. The other firefighters had moved farther away, leaving the three of them relatively isolated. Stepping behind a crumbling and charred wall, the woman grabbed a sharpened piece of un-melted metal, readied herself, and called to Bill. "Hey, come here a sec'. There's something here I want to show you."

Bill smirked. Sooner or later, they all wanted him. "Coming, sweetheart," he said, sidestepping blackened debris as he unknowingly approached his final destination.

Cat Russell

The Field Trip

Kate clutched her sketchbook in her arms and stared. The way the sculptor brought life to stone always amazed her. The girl with roses in her hair seemed so *real*. She reached out with one hand to touch the cold lips but pulled back reflexively when the Professor called her.

"Kay!" he shouted across the room. "Anytime now, hon'. The rest of the class has moved on, but if you like we can *all* wait on you."

Jerk, Why does he have to embarrass me in front of everyone? Kate thought. She answered, "Sorry, I'm coming!" Crossing the room, she ignored the eyes of her peers to glance back at the marble maiden. *Did she just move?*

No, she answered herself. *I must be stressed. I'm seeing things.*

The empty eyes of the ivory girl followed her.

Kate looked at the postcard, remembering the field trip. She'd always loved the museum. She went as often as possible, especially since college students didn't need to pay. Roaming the granite halls, she spent hours lost in paintings, plaster, and marble. But something about this particular statue piqued her interest. Since its arrival only the month previous, she'd been somewhat obsessed with it. She fantasized that the stone girl wanted to tell her something, if only Kate could reach her. She imagined the right strokes on pale paper breaking a spell and bringing her to life.

She wasn't a great artist, which she admitted to anyone that asked. Nevertheless, she signed up for every drawing, painting, or other creative class she could. She wasn't bad. She just wasn't very good. The idea of bringing to life an idea or story had always attracted her. Maybe her current fixation was just her mind's way of telling herself to try her hand at sculpture. Maybe that would reveal hidden talent, buried inside, waiting to be unleashed by chisel and hammer.

She took another quick look before pinning the photo to the wall. She compared her sketch with the photo. Her graphite roses seemed off, and the girl's chin wasn't quite right. There was something missing in her expression, something sad and nameless in the eyes. Well, maybe she'd get it right later or go back tomorrow. Yes, that was the answer. How accurate could she be from just a photo? It was silly, but she felt the girl deserved better.

The next day, Kate stepped off the bus, adjusted her pack, and walked through the museum. She'd meant to come earlier in the day, when the lighting was better, but she'd missed the bus. A friend offered her a ride, then backed out, and after heated words she found herself at the bus stop again. The museum would close soon. There was hardly any point in coming at all.

She walked straight to the statue, looked in its eyes, then pulled a stool from out of the corner. She pulled out her sketchbook and pencil and began to draw.

Free me…

Kate looked up from the pad in her hand. The girl in the statue said nothing. She looked around at the nearly empty room. Patrons were slowly filing out. *It must be someone else,* Kate thought, bending to her task once more.

Free me…

She looked up quickly. Did she see those eyes blink? *I must be going mad,* she scolded herself. She pulled her shawl around her more closely and swore off soda for a week. Too much caffeine played tricks with your mind. She stared at the girl for a full minute before turning her gaze downward.

When the light began to dim, she looked up suddenly, shocked out of her reverie. Moving the number 2 in her hand, dusting off the rubber trail of her eraser, smudging the lines on creamy paper had taken her out of time. She had felt nothing and seen no one except the ivory-faced girl and the results of her own labor.

She sat alone in the darkened room, empty of all save herself, the stone girl, and a dozen other statues.

A figure came around the corner, stopping to look at Kate.

"What are you still doing here, little girl?" he asked. She winced at the voice behind her. She hated jabs about her age.

"Sorry, sir. I lost track of time. I didn't mean to stay past closing," Kate called back, hurriedly packing her things and slinging her bag over her shoulder. She turned to face the man stepping out of the shadows.

"Professor Alpha? I didn't know…" her voice trailed off. *What was he doing here? Moonlighting?*

"You know, I knew the moment I saw you that you were just what I needed," he said, advancing slowly. Kate retreated involuntarily, her back pressed against the flowing frozen folds of the maiden's gown. The stone lent her strength. No stalker was going to push her around!

"Wow," she said, reaching down into her half-closed bag, "I knew you were a rotten teacher. I didn't know you were a pervert." She gripped the pencil tightly in her hand, hidden from his view.

"Is that what you think?" he smirked.

Suddenly, Kate felt cold hands on her shoulders. Her spine turned to ice water as she heard the thoughts whispered in her ear.

Free me…

"Hate to tell you this, girly, but I'm not the one you should be afraid of."

Kate stood, paralyzed with fear.

"You thought you chose her? You wanted to bring her to life!" His smile sliced her in two. "Well, then today's your lucky day."

Dread welled in her as she felt, more than heard, his next words.

"Because *she* chose *you*."

The man and the young girl held hands as they left the statue behind in the darkened room. The empty eyes seemed to follow them, along with a silent sob.

Free me.

Cat Russell

Ghost of a Chance

I stare from the crack in the closet door with a mixture of horror and ice-cold rage. The stranger rifles through dresser drawers, throwing delicates on the floor in an attempt to find other valuables. As if he hasn't taken enough. His dark backpack sits open on the floor next to him, filled with the things he has already stolen from me. I feel I should be more scared of what comes next, but outrage pushes all other thoughts from my mind.

How dare he break into my home.

The man pushes back long bangs before slamming the last drawer in frustration. He turns and views my bruised and broken body. He strokes his chin and bites his lips ragged as he prints his frustration with bloody boot prints across the floor. Finally, he grabs my limp and lifeless arms and drags me to the bathroom across the hall. He dumps my body in the tub and leaves the room.

I can't leave, can't move. I can't escape this prison of flesh and bone he's trapped me in. I hear my killer move in other rooms, cabinets open and shut, bottles shuffling, the sound of metal on metal as my murderer looks for a way to dispose of the evidence of his crime.

When he returns, he pauses a moment in the doorway, staring. He hadn't really looked before. The attack had been so unexpected, both for him and for me. I'd felt his panicked blow on the back of my head, my brain battered into unconsciousness before I could turn and see his face. When I awoke to new form, he was busy shoving my remains into the nearest closet. He had avoided my gaze before, as though unable to face what he had done, but that careful avoidance was over now.

His face is close to mine, a hair's breadth from my own. I feel his warm breath on my rapidly cooling skin, his panic replaced by a calculated examination of my face as he weighs his options, how to cover his tracks. Finally, his gaze reaches my lifeless eyes, the eyes I've been trapped behind.

He stares into them, penetrating them with his scrutiny. That meeting, that shared connection, is all I need. We see each other completely, soul to soul.

And that is all I need to call upon my power.

He recoils in terror, bone white with dawning horror…not for what he's done, but for what I am doing to him as we change places.

The ability I've struggled to hide all my life finally serves me well in death. My old life may be over, but my new one has just begun.

As I consider the best method of disposing of my corpse, I can't help but smile. I know he watches me watching him behind those dead eyes, wondering what horrors lay in store, imprisoned within my former body. I know he must be terrified.

Serves the bastard right.

Cat Russell

Blood

The Count of La Rue Morgue sneered at his servant as the zombie entered, carrying the wine glass filled with dark, thick liquid. "You may go, Alfred." The servant shuffled through the stone archway to the adjoining kitchen, within earshot should his Master call again. "It's impossible to find good help these days," said the Count, wiping crimson stains from the white lace of his shirt.

Laughter cut through the silence like shards of broken glass. "It's impossible to imagine them ever leading a revolt against the aristocracy," said the Countess. "Their only brains are the ones they eat!"

Another creature said, "Don't be so sure, my lady. The nobles of France thought the same thing before they lost their heads, did they not?"

"Oh, don't remind me," muttered the Count. "I'm still ambivalent about that revolution. All that glorious blood! But the rabble rising to overthrow their betters… The thought still sickens me."

"Perhaps it's not wise to keep so many," said another guest. "Intelligent or not, we can still be outnumbered."

Now it was the Countess's turn to scoff. "Indeed! As if they would want what is in our heads! They only crave grey matter, Geoffrey, and living grey matter at that. What would a dull-witted beast want from the emptying of our skulls?"

Revenge, thought Alfred, sharpening another blade.

Brothers

The pale figure scratched his head with one taloned hand and regarded his brother. "Igor," it said.

"Boris," said the other creature, stepping from the shadows. "I knew you'd come back here eventually."

"I could say the same about you," Boris replied. Moonlight reflected off the surface of his marble skin.

Igor approached, though not a single leaf crunched beneath his feet. "Can you blame me? This was our home… long ago. "

The other creature's stillness remained unbroken. Electricity charged the atmosphere. The wind sang a mournful tune through trees whose leafy garments lay strewn upon the ground. After a few moments, Boris said, "I do."

"I had no choice. The plague would have taken you. It was the only way."

"Save my life by taking it? How can I thank you, brother?" No warmth lingered in his eyes for the companion of his ancient childhood.

"I sickened too. Our kind cannot consume infected blood without some risk. I almost died the true death."

"What a comfort that was as I fought to survive the wound you gave me." He touched the scar on his neck.

"What can I do?" Igor asked.

"Finish what the plague started. Never again will you inflict this monstrosity on another to stave off your own weakness." He grinned. "Don't worry, old friend. I promise to be more merciful than you were to me. I will only kill you."

Cat Russell

Collection

The young man's voice, almost lost in the roar of an unseen wind, rose with the final incantation. The candle flames flared and died, immersing the room in darkness. From within the circle, a feeble voice called, "Billy?"

The boy, almost a man, called out, "Just a sec', Uncle Bubba." He ran to a corner and flipped a switch. Electric brilliance illuminated the garage. The corpse shielded its eyes until Billy fitted it with a grease-stained baseball cap, identical to the one he wore himself. "There," he said. "Better?"

A single bulb hung from the garage ceiling, like a noose, casting the clutter that surrounded the circle into sharp relief. The cadaver gazed at the detritus of its former life and extended one pale, decomposing hand towards its nephew. "Whyyyyy?" it moaned.

Billy laughed and shrugged off the creature's grip like so many dead leaves. "Hey, you know why. We need your pension money. Here, sign these." He shoved a pen and some paperwork in front of his uncle.

The creature grabbed the pen and scrawled its signature with difficulty. Then it looked to Billy.

The young man laughed again—a cold, hard sound. "Oh, no you don't, Bubba," he said. "I'm not through with you. Not yet." The creature recoiled. "You were a bastard in life, and now that the money's taken care of, there's time for payback." He picked up a shovel. "I'm betting you still feel pain. The first time I used this, you died too quick." He grinned, exposing his crooked, yellow teeth. "This time," he said, "I plan to make it last."

A Match Made in the Heavens

She can't get over the look in his eyes. Well, are they technically *his* eyes when they belong to the humanoids looking through his rounded glass portholes, eyes enormous with unmitigated terror? It doesn't matter. She is used to that reaction from most lifeforms, whether they have one set of eyes or many.

What do you want me to do, my love? she thinks to the ship in dragonsong.

The ship roars his response, but the dragon hears nothing through the void of space from which she comes. She only knows that she loves this gleaming metal creature sailing across the starry heavens, loves looking at the faces of the humanoid creatures he apparently swallowed, loves the electric fire shining off his exterior.

They have so much in common!

Then she sees where the vessel, the lovely silver knight of her nights, is heading and her thoughts fairly explode in her head for joy. The frosty silence of the void is replaced by the roaring heat of entry into the planet's atmosphere; they are the match that ignites the heavens. Approaching the planet's dark side, she spots his love offering to her: a city that sparkles and glints like a nest of jewels across the ground's surface.

Telepathy or not, it is as if her beloved can read her thoughts. They sail together towards the world, a world where they can finally and truly speak. The planet's oxygen-rich atmosphere fills her lungs, her wings whoosh through the air as she rapidly descends to view the brightly lit buildings that litter the ground like fallen stars.

Upon closer inspection, small circular windows in each metallic dome reveal more tiny humanoids. This must be his home, the place he's taken her to feast…

Oh what bliss! The creatures flee from their dwellings, feet pounding furiously as they run for their lives, and she picks them off one by one, savoring each morsel as the love offering it is obviously meant to be—like tiny bipedal chocolates that scream sweet harmonies as she gulps each one down.

Running her long, forked tongue along scaled lips, she sways provocatively toward the ship that now sits parked like a gleaming silver tooth. Her back undulates, her eyes sparkle, and her nostrils flare as she inhales deeply the sweet stench of burning meat. She folds each set of iridescent wings slowly, as though dancing a ballet of death in this beautiful and burning world. She is surprised to find the ground still cool to her touch, as she crunches concrete beneath clawed, blue-white digits.

They had sailed the heavens together, her and her lover. He had brought her to dinner. Now, it is time for her to show how deeply she feels their connection. Her heart swells with happiness. With the high-pitched wails of dying humanoids to accompany her song, she fills her lungs with fire, her throat with blazing verse, and prepares to show her lover how hotly her passion truly burns.

DragonKind Love

Princess Serina, how lovely to see you.

Thank you, the young woman replied, careful to aim deliberate conscious thought at the creature. She stood straight, swallowed the dust in her mouth, and looked the beast in the eye. Dragon-thought was always disarming: an unwanted but necessary intimacy between their species—barring the invention of a universal translator. She couldn't *wait* for that. The creature probed her mind. Her subconscious felt as naked and vulnerable as her forebears had been, back in barbarous times when human royalty would sacrifice them to this creature's ancestors; first born females were always prized as the tastiest, the juiciest. She wondered if they still thought that.

There is no need for apprehension, your Highness, answered the creature, the mental intrusion clawing at the corners of her mind. *We have a freshly inked treaty, remember? And I assure you, we haven't eaten humans for ages. In fact, my clan follows a mostly vegetarian diet.*

Dammit! She needed to keep better control than this. This was a friendly meeting between their two kingdoms, but there was also a reason first-borns were kept in the dark about state matters. No matter how well trained, it was impossible to hide all your thoughts from a telepath—even well-meaning ones. She needed to keep her cool, even if some of her private thoughts were a bit embarrassing.

You are correct, my dear, replied the ambassador, her emerald green eyes softening their gaze at the slightly trembling creature before her. *I know you are unused to our method of communication, but I want to assure you that I will not read any further into your mind than you wish. If you let the occasional private thought slip, I will make no mention of it. It's common courtesy.*

Serina relaxed, letting go of the breath she hadn't

realized she had been holding. The creature was beautiful, if terrifying. Several stories tall, at least, with iridescent scales the color of her ancestors blood and—stop it, stop it, STOP IT.

The creature smiled, revealing long cruel fangs. *Well, we might as well get onto business. Shall we begin with the tour of our facility?*

Serina nodded and followed the creature down surprisingly bright hallways. The mountain caverns had been hollowed out ages ago, the walls polished to a shine. The antiseptic glow of fluorescent lights led them to the main assembly chamber, a room that opened up into the heart of the mountain, its floor far below and its ceiling far above her head. Dragons bustled between the machines, operating various equipment. She felt like an ant trapped in a beehive.

A matte blue dragon holding a clipboard finished instructing a few young drakes in the operation of some machinery and flew up to join them, grinning wildly. *Princess Serina! How lovely to meet you. I can't tell you how excited we all are about today's demonstration!* His enormous bulk filled her vision as he approached.

Visions of her ancestors chained to rocks, waiting to be devoured, filled her brain.

Princess! His cheerful demeanor faltered. *I would never—*

The red dragon shot the blue a look and, amazingly, his thoughts were replaced by hers in Serina's head.

I apologize for my mate. In his excitement, he sometimes oversteps the bounds of courtesy, but I assure you he means well. May I introduce you to the creator and subject of today's demonstration, my mate?

Serina curtsied, pulling the sides of her long gown outward as she bent. *Nice to meet you*, she thought. She would never get used to creatures introducing each other without names. She supposed in a telepathic society, there was probably no need for them. But wait, did he think—

Subject? What did you mean subject of the demonstration? She was either getting the hang of directed thought or her hosts were too polite to point out her deficiencies.

The blue's eyes glinted, his smile returned. *I can't wait to show you our facility! I've been director of research here for years, and now that we're finally allies, I can't WAIT to show you the progress we've made on 3D printing!*

She ignored her uneasiness and smiled back. He seemed genuine enough. They both did. Then again, with creatures so alien to her experience, how would she know? And if they had something up their sleeves…claws?…there was absolutely nothing she could do about it anyway. Humanity had always been at a disadvantage against dragonkind. Their sheer size was intimidating, their ability to breathe fire horrifying, and their civilization so advanced that humans were like insects to them. The treaty was purely a goodwill gesture on the dragons' part. They could squash her and her city like bugs beneath their claws if they so wished. But their civilization had evolved over time to detest violence against defenseless creatures like humans. Thank the gods for that. Still, in the back of her mind, she wondered if they were just letting the population rise enough for the next culling. Farmers never killed all their livestock at once; they had to let them breed to keep up the inventory.

We need to descend to the factory floor for the demonstration, your Highness, thought Red. *I'm afraid…we don't have elevators or steps.*

Serina nodded and stepped onto the red dragon's outstretched claw, sitting on the leathery palm's surface, propped against the creature's curled digits as though reclining in a LazyGirl. It was the bravest thing she'd ever done.

Red cradled her palm against her chest, careful not

to squeeze too tightly as she flew to the floor with her mate. Serina wondered why they didn't simply jump down but realized that the flight was in deference to her: a jump would have jostled her more in the creature's palm than a smooth landing from a short flight. She relaxed. Slightly.

Blue's exuberance had returned. He showed her the machines, massive silver and gold monstrosities inset with jewels. While Blue explained their practicalities, demonstrating how everyday materials could be created via the 3D printing process, Red explained that functionality and beauty always went together in dragon culture.

I know this is probably a ridiculous question, but aren't you worried about printing weapons? She directed the thought at both creatures.

They laughed, full-throated guttural guffaws that echoed off the cavern walls. She waited for them to stop. She waited quite a while.

My dear, thought Red, *as I've assured all the humans I've met, we are an entirely peaceful society. We no longer prey on helpless creatures. And even if we did, we are allies. I assure you, we have no reservations about sharing—within limits—our technology. For instance, we can now…well…*

Blue recognized his cue and thought, *We can now print ORGANS.*

Serina's eyes widened. *What?!*

We've had cloning technology for a while now, continued Red, *the ability to use a small amount of a creature's cells to grow an exact genetic duplicate. We've experimented with ways to accelerate growth, etc., but without much luck until recently. This new track, however, marries cloning technology with 3D printing.*

We basically multiply the cells we need to be used as ink for the printer, thought Blue. *I'm going to give you a demonstration using some of my own cells.* With surprising precision, Blue used his claw to cut a small square swatch of skin from his palm. He inserted it in the massive machine. *It doesn't matter what section of my body the cells come from; the DNA works with the printing technology to create whatever type of cell is needed. If I wanted a kidney, I could have it clone a kidney from the cells of my palm. It's quite exciting!*

Red added, *But my mate has planned an even more impressive demonstration. We realize you are largely ignorant of our culture, and he wisely thought to blend the technological aspects of our little tour along with some social ones. The printing is fast, but it will still be several hours before it's complete.*

She smiled. *That's why our tour will now continue to our eating space. Except for special occasions, we have group meals, as having shared time with shared experiences is important in any family.*

Family? thought Serina. *I thought this facility was run by your government.*

Well, yes and no, answered Blue. *Our kingdom is large, but is not a kingdom an extended family? You have your closest relatives—mothers and sons and so forth, then cousins, then distant cousins, extending to all your country and your species, no? It's no different for us, except that we acknowledge our common kinship more openly.*

Just then, they arrived at the communal dining area. Serina, upon learning she was to share a meal with her hosts, was apprehensive at first. Her fears, however, were soon laid to rest. A huge smoking cauldron, larger than the dining hall in her own castle, stood over a fire in the center of the enormous room. Dragons came and went, using the ladle to help themselves to the steaming concoction inside. Whatever it was, it smelled delicious.

Since the bowls they used were far too big for a human to carry, Red filled and handed what appeared to be an appropriately-sized bowl to the young woman. She looked around for something to drink and was handed a similar bowl filled with the sweetest ale she had ever tried. They placed her on top of a large copper colored table; she was the same size as their salt shaker. Still, she enjoyed the brew as she got up the nerve to try the stew. She noted the other dragons drinking ale from oversized bottles; she was not entirely surprised when she realized her bowls were bottle caps.

Red and Blue had served themselves and sat at the table. *What do you think of the meal?* asked Blue.

The ale is wonderful, Serina answered.

What about the stew? asked Red, green eyes twinkling. She had been sipping from her bowl, and the corners of her mouth revealed red-stained teeth.

Serina knew Red was teasing her; she also knew she needed to eat the stew. It did smell heavenly, but she was afraid to imagine what went into it. For all the dragons' peaceful claims, she couldn't help suspecting it contained man flesh. Wasn't human flesh supposed to taste like pork? Tales of savage cannibals claimed it was called long pig and, and—she needed to get her thoughts under control: directed or not. Gods know she didn't want to put those thoughts in their heads.

She lifted the bowl and sipped. Her hosts watched her tip the bowl more, biting into the chunky bits of stew that made it to the bowl's edge. The stew was delicious. Was she a cannibal now? Setting the bowl down, she wiped her chin with the back of her hand. It came away red.

So how do you like the borscht? asked Red.

Blue had already finished his bowl and gone back for seconds.

I asked them to make it special today, because it's my mate's favorite meal. Today's such a special day for him.

I understand he's been working on this project for so long. He's the main developer, yes?

Yes, and today is the first time he's used his own cells in the printer. It's like welcoming a new member into our family.

Before Serina could ask Red to elaborate, Blue returned to the table, all smiles, his bowl already half-emptied. When everyone in the cavern had eaten their fill, they chatted until someone started to sing. Dragon song, unlike human song, was a mixture of the telepathic and what sounded like harp music emanating from dragon throats instead of acid-tinged fire. As the poetry of a hundred souls filled her mind, she closed her eyes. She knew she would never know another moment like this one, so pure, so without malice or envy, just joy. It was the most beautiful thing she had ever experienced. All her apprehensions melted away.

When the song was over, Blue took up his favorite subject again, describing the many applications of 3D printing technology now that it included the organic: printed replacement organs for organ transplants, new arms or legs for those mutilated in accidents or born without, even food could be printed.

Food? asked Serina. The dragon song has quelled her fears as to their intentions, but who knew what they meant by that word? Just because they didn't eat humans anymore, there was no reason to think other things unpalatable to the human tongue might be on the menu. Still, beet stew was Blue's favorite meal…

Don't worry, replied Red, *the beets were from our garden. We have a hydroponics lab.*

Hours passed with Blue chatting away, and Red filling in the gaps in Serina's understanding. By the time they returned to the factory floor, Serina could not wait to see the results of the demonstration. A new Blue? How did that work?

They walked out, the three of them, and viewed the silent monstrosity before them.

It looks like…a statue, thought Serina. Her face

fell.

It might as well be, until the process is complete, said Red. *Don't worry. It'll become clear soon.*

Serina stood back, waiting. What else could she do?

My mate uploaded a backup of his personality to the computer before your arrival. He's been doing regular scans for months, in preparation, Red explained.

Serina nodded, uncomprehending.

Blue walked over and hit some buttons on an oversized console. Blue's silent doppelganger began to glow slightly, and there was a hiss of ozone and electricity. The creature opened his eyes.

Blue ran over and embraced his duplicate in an enormous hug that would have crushed a creature other than…well, himself. The creature hugged back, then locked eyes with Red. *Is it time?* he asked.

Almost, answered Red. Serina guessed that even though the question was not directed at her, the dragons had included her as one of their many courtesies. Red nodded to her mate—her original mate, and he walked over, suddenly shy.

Serina watched the creatures carefully, knowing she would need to remember details for her debriefing. Posterity would remember this historic encounter between their two species. She appreciated Red and Blue allowing her to overhear…overthink? their conversation. The factory floor, filled with gleaming machines, as well as the four of them, suddenly seemed so intimate. She felt like an eavesdropper. Maybe she was. Had they forgotten her?

The printed Blue…BluePrint, she mentally dubbed him with a chuckle, walked over to stand near her and give his progenitor and Red some privacy, though Serina wasn't sure what constituted privacy in this telepathic world. Still, the couple standing just a few feet away did seem to forget them, lost in each other's gazes.

I love you, thought Red, tracing one claw along her

mate's face.

I know, I love you too, thought Blue, covering that claw with his own. He smiled and closed his eyes.

Very gently, almost reverently, Red inserted her claw deep into her mate's skull. There was almost no blood, just a slight leakage from his auditory hole as he slid noiselessly into her arms. She licked each of his eyes with care, her forked tongue leaving her saliva along the lids—a dragon's kiss, before laying him on the ground.

Serina watched, speechless.

Then Red turned to Blue's doppelganger and hugged him tightly. *Welcome to the family, my love.*

"What the hell just happened?!" cried Serina, forgetting all her training, all her composure, even that the words themselves were meaningless to dragons uninstructed in her human tongue.

It didn't matter. Her thoughts resonated with the words, and even if they had not, her tone conveyed all.

Red wiped one smoking tear from her eye before composing herself and turning to her guest. Blue Number Two stood beside her.

I'm sorry for your discomfort, she said. *We probably should have explained this part more, but—as you can understand—this is an intimate ritual. Letting a human witness this…it's the ultimate honor.*

Serina backed away, mouth working over unspoken words.

You see, Red continued, holding onto Blue Two's claw as if for strength. *I am with children. My nutritional requirements quadruple during pregnancy, and my children need the extra calories. My mate gave his life to nurture his children.* She squeezed Two's claw in her own.

Serina stared.

It has always been this way for Dragonkind, picked up Two. *No other food will satisfy the little ones but the flesh of their father. The only difference is, this time—*

This time, finished Red, gazing with love at the printed copy beside her, *my children get to be raised by their father as well as their mother. We get to keep him.*

In a way, said Two.

And Serina, gods help her, began to see what they meant. She looked at the body laying peacefully just a few feet away. It steamed slightly, a dragon's corpse losing its heat to the surrounding area. And though she knew that Two wasn't the one that had died, she couldn't resist asking—both with thought and word, "*But how could you let her kill you?*"

Blue smiled again that terrifying toothy grin, a smile she recognized, and replied, *What parent wouldn't sacrifice their life for their children?*

Where there be Dragons

The sight on his weapon brought them into closer range, dazzling his eyes. Sunlight glinted off scales as it lowered its head to feed its hungry brood. *Must be a female*, he thought, *that'll bring extra.*

He couldn't believe fellow spacers still believed in magic, ha! All he cared about was what he could see with his eyes and feel in his hand, namely golden scales, precious stones, and the warm ichor that fetched a high price with any of the dark magicians.

It was mostly superstition that kept people at bay from these "gentle giants," what the local bleeding hearts called them. He wouldn't be surprised to find that the damned environmentalists had started the whole uproar about magic and sentience.

The beast walked into the cave, followed by her brood, out of sight and out of range.

He cursed silently. His research showed that they liked to sun themselves while they slept, and he'd hoped to catch them napping. A shot to the eyes (their least protected spot, even through the gold lids) at close range when they were unawares. The hatchlings were blind as newborn puppies; they'd be no problem. He could tranq them easily, then pack and ship 'em. Money in the bank.

So much for that plan.

Luckily the females typically raised the young alone most of the time. He knew that no male dragons had been sighted here since mating season, so it was unlikely daddy would show up to spoil the fun. Dabbing some dragon urine on his neck, an unpleasant if necessary precaution, he quickly packed his gear and crept to the cave entrance.

The mother dragon curled on the floor with her little ones snuggled against her belly, tail wound protectively around them. Mothers were fierce and unpredictable, so he'd need to make sure she remained unaware of him. He scanned the inside of the cave for signs of other dragons. None presented themselves, and he crept forward.

Without warning, he felt his feet yanked from under him. His weapon clattered to the ground, metal on stone, as he hung from the ceiling like a chicken ready for slaughter. He couldn't believe his eyes. The dragon was staring at him, her voice sounding in his head.

Did you think you'd outwit me, hunter?, she said.

Telepathy? Telekinesis? Dammit. Everyone knew those traits were reserved for certain, gifted humans. Cunning, crafty, yes. But telekinesis? It served him right for underestimating his prey.

I am glad that you showed up though, she told him.

He dangled there and waited. There was nothing else he could do, held as he was in the firm grip of her mind. He saw her blind brats nuzzling the jewels along her stomach. Their cries pierced the cave walls.

Why is that? asked the man. He didn't know if she could hear him, but it was worth a shot.

Because my children are hungry. He felt himself propelled along the ceiling to hang above the three hungry hatchlings.

No! You can't be serious! his mind screamed.

She smiled, something he'd never realized dragons could do. *Of course not,* she whispered in his head. *We prefer other fare.*

Like what? his mind cried. Somehow he'd lost the ability to speak.

She smiled. *Chocolate.*

He recovered his voice. "Chocolate? CHOCOLATE? WHAT THE HELL…?"

She smiled wider, revealing multiple rows of sharp

teeth. *You wouldn't guess it from our anatomy, but chocolate sustains us quite nicely.*

He swallowed hard.

I think it's the sugar rush.

He tried to swallow again while he recovered himself. What kind of game was she playing? He was a hunter, dammit! He'd be damned if he'd be toyed with by a serpentine beast with a sweet tooth.

If you're going to eat me, go ahead, he thought savagely, *I'd rather have it over with than hang here like some sort of demonic chew toy…*

Hearty, bellowing laughter filled the cave. She snorted a few times before finally getting herself under control.

Oh, I'm sorry, she said, *Well, no, not really. But I'll give you an opportunity. If you promise to get us some chocolate, I'll let you go.*

Incredulity filled him. *That's it? And…?*

And what? I need to feed my children. You're not much of a threat, it's true, but I'd rather not be annoyed by you in the future.

What happens if I don't do it?

If you agree and break your word, I'll find you. And you'll be very, very sorry.

What if I say no?

I'll just kill you now.

But I thought you didn't eat people.

Who said I was going to eat you?

The hunter mulled this over. He could agree and bring the chocolates back to the beast. He could also hop in his spacer and simply fly away.

I've already disabled your ship. The dragon slowly turned, careful not to disturb her children. She pulled some warped metal from a side passage.

How did you…?

She looked at him.

So…you let me go, and I get your chocolate. When I bring it back, you'll let me leave again, but this time for good?

Almost, she told him, *You also must swear to never hunt our kind again. After our bargain is fulfilled, I'll allow you to leave this world. Understand?*

The hunter agreed to her terms. She could watch him in the village, so he'd obey. He'd eventually catch a lift with some passing trader and escape this rock. Then he could return in force to teach her and her brats a lesson.

She smiled as his shadow cut a sharp outline against the snowy background. Her hatchlings were hungry.

Don't worry, darlings, she said. *Dinner is coming soon, and this time he's bringing dessert.*

Sea Life

The blue dress uniforms co-opted from the Navy were itchy. The sailors imprisoned within them were tired and hot and couldn't wait for the ceremony to be over. The captain looked across the water at the setting sun. At least this would soon be over, and they'd get some respite from this day's infernal heat. But yet…

He looked down into the cool depths of the ocean waters surrounding the metal monstrosity he had called his home for the better part of three years. The setting sun glowed gold and orange upon the waves. He shuddered.

"And do you, Mark Wallace, take this mermaid, Jasmine Petals, to be your lawfully wedded wife? In sickness and in health…forever and ever, by Neptune's salty bits?"

The young sailor looked down at the mermaid clinging to the ship's side, gulped, and nodded his head. The red-haired beauty in the crystal blue waters smiled her approval, exposing sharp incisors in her delicate, full-lipped mouth.

"By the eternal laws of the sea, by Neptune's trident and Amphitrite's coral crown, I now pronounce you mer-man and mer-wife. The bride may now—-"

With a stupendous leap, the new bride pulled her husband over the edge of the warship, dragging him along with her as she splashed into the waters below. Soon, not even the emerald green of her tail could be seen as she brought the new merman to her lair in the deep dark waters.

The men and women shook their heads in wonder. There was a reason humans steered clear of Neptune's children. The mermaid's kiss might cure their fellow sailor's cancer, but the cure might just be worse than the disease.

Captain Deadly allowed himself a rare sigh of pity for his former crewman before ordering his crew to hoist the Jolly Roger. Fresh plunder lay ahead, and he might need the gold. Who knew? In his own future, he might need to hire an oncologist.

Trapped

From my pilot's seat, I watch the contents of the aquarium tank strapped to the plane's inner wall. My cargo's withstood shipment far better than I anticipated. Mermen bodies are less valuable dead than alive, so I'm glad I took extra precautions to ensure this package is cared for properly. Thank the gods I had the vet sedate him before shipment. Though the tank is shatter-resistant, I wouldn't want to test it; if he becomes violent, he might damage himself.

Usually, men alone track mermen, but their rarity coupled with their ferocity makes capturing them almost impossible. No one expects a woman to bag such a vicious creature. But it pays to know the science. By synthesizing mermaid pheromones, I'm able to use them to my advantage. I'm actually surprised how easy it was to lure the thing into a cage.

Still, he is a handsome beast. The way his emerald hair floats in the tank's water, the way his sea-green eyes sparkle—

He's watching me.

He's watching me, capturing me in the depths of those startling eyes.

I feel myself change course, away from land and back towards the sea. My hands are moving; I feel the plane's weight shift now that the nose is aimed for those beautiful, calm waters.

The merman lifts himself from his tank. I smell salt air and realize just how wrong I've been about everything.

Cat Russell

Hot Librarian

One hundred feet was all that separated them. Kenny surveyed the otherworldly creature: long glossy hair, sparkling eyes, gleaming teeth. Sweating a river, he swallowed, felt his heart beating against his chest like a convict on the bars of his prison cell. Wiping his sleeve across his damp forehead, he forced himself to approach. He would face his fate like a man--sexism be damned!-even if it killed him. With his social skills, he'd likely die of embarrassment anyway.

"Excuse me," he said to the lone librarian.

She turned penetrating green eyes on him, eyes that would have terrified a thousand schoolchildren with the mere idea of a scolding, eyes that bored into his soul from behind thick black rims and bifocal lenses. Those emerald orbs looked him up and down like a cat examining its dinner. "Yes?" she answered. A smile curled the corners of full pink lips; she watched him squirm beneath her gaze.

"I…," replied Kenny. He prayed for a heart attack to end his torment.

Her grin widened, revealing slightly uneven teeth. This close, he noticed freckles scattered across her nose like assorted tic tacs. Her imperfections increased his desire as he realized he was being absurd. She was a person--not some*thing* to be fawned over, but someone he could talk to. He was being ridiculous, he could–

"Would you go out with me?" The question erupted from his mouth before his brain could catch up.

Her eyes grew larger, then lit up as her mouth widened into a lopsided grin. "I'm…working. Right now."

"Later then? When do you get off?" His mouth had decided to go solo, but since things were going well his brain didn't seem to mind.

"In a few minutes actu-actually, but, but the library

is closing, I was just about to lock up. I need to ch-ch-change sssso you'd better go…for now. Right now."

A stutter? Adorable!

"That's okay. I'll wait." Way to go, mouth. But wait, why was *she* nervous? She liked him a minute ago. Was she trying to get rid of him?

"I'm Kenny, by the way. And you are…?" His mouth was on autopilot now.

The librarian hurried to the door, jingling a large metal ring of keys conspicuously near the waist of her pencil skirt.

"Betty. I'm so-so-sorrrrrry but go nnnoOWWWWLLLL!" She screamed loud and long, and bent double, clutching her abdomen. She grabbed Kenny for support, her face contorted with…pain? Could pain stretch the skin across her face like--

"Holy crap!" cried Kenny, struggling to pry her nails from his arm. As Betty performed the type of bodily stretches even yoga instructors avoided, he extricated himself from her grasp. He watched her transform, horrified; her enormous lupine body now blocked his only exit. He knew he should run, bolt, hide, but his legs refused to move.

The wolf turned emerald green eyes on Kenny, towered over his quivering form, and…smiled? It was hard to tell with her thick pink tongue hanging out and all the drool.

"Damn, I'm so embarrassed!" growled Betty, sloppy tears leaking from eyes the size of tennis balls. "I meet a nice guy and *transform* in front of him! I can't believe I—uh, did you…?" Her elongated nose sniffed his crotch, where a large dark stain spread. Ashamed, she pulled back her nose. "Sorry about…*that*."

Was she was apologizing for the sniff or the leak?

"It's not exactly first date stuff," she said, meekly. At least, he thought she did; she was talking through a mouth full of teeth and tongue.

This was too much, even for Kenny. He edged toward the door when she shifted position. "Okay, I see you're really busy tonight. You warned me! I mean, I didn't think you meant *changing* changing, know what I mean, but no hard feelings, I'll get out and leave you ahhh…lone?" He viewed her ripped clothes; the pencil skirt split down the middle, had landed on an endcap of supernatural romances.

Fate was just plain mean.

"Oh, I'm sorry! It's just bad timing, isn't it?" Remarkably, she spoke more clearly. Were-Betty fumbled with the keys in the door, her claws making the simple task cumbersome, but finally she held the door wide. "I'm so embarrassed. These winter hours! It gets dark so soon, I'm just blathering, aren't I? I'll just stay in, catch up on my graphic novels, and—"

"Graphic novels?" said Kenny, one foot out the door. "You read graphic novels?"

"Well, yeah. I know I could read the comics individually, but I like binge-reading. I special ordered the newest *Walking Dead*, so—"

"Wait, you read *The Walking Dead*?" said Kenny, pausing despite himself. This was an aspect of the library he had frankly never considered.

"Sure! I can show you what we have but, uh, don't you want to…?" She waved one long paw in the direction of his dampened pants. He noticed her nose curl and felt responsible, petrified, *mortified*.

"Maybe when you come back tomorrow I can show you?" Betty looked like she was batting her eyes at him. It was disturbing.

No one was perfect though, right? Where was he going to find a hot librarian that liked comics *and* him? Kenny shrank again. *What was he thinking?* He couldn't come back here! Maybe he'd phone up with a fake voice, ask for a loan through the mail or—

"Again, so sorry. Just go. I'll use your library info to email you how to check out the digital comics."

Kenny bolted.

She didn't blame him. How could she? She would, of course, track him; though her nose was sufficient, there was no need to resort to something that crude. She'd use the library's technology. Besides, she'd noticed the fresh scratches on his arm. A month was plenty of time for him to get used to the idea of her condition--as well as his own. He'd be back. After all, he'd need answers. What better place to get them than the library?

Cat Russell

Quietus

The worst thing about the zombie apocalypse was the damned unicorns. It was easy enough to escape human zombies; they were slow moving and chronically uncoordinated creatures with very little brain power of their own. Perhaps that was why they hungered for the grey matter of others.

The first time Maggie saw an infected unicorn its matted, yellowing fur, dead eyes, and hideous pink mane made her skin crawl, and that was simply from the color scheme. Its blood-soaked horn was even more gruesome, though not much. However, it had gored some hippies instead of her, so she'd counted her blessings and moved on.

Too soon, as it turned out, because she'd failed to consider one thing. Zombie unicorns were fast. They didn't have wings, but they didn't need them. Their feet could trample you in seconds flat, and then the creature could simply lick up grey matter gumbo for its dinner. She'd barely escaped by turning into an alley too narrow for the beast to follow.

After a few minutes, the menacing fiend whinnied and returned to its meal of mashed hippie. She was left alone with her thoughts, most of them unpleasant. She figured it must belong to the herd that escaped from the local Crypto-zoo. She wondered if their caretakers had died from the virus or a goring.

Over time, unicorn sightings became more frequent within the ruined city. Even worse, the animals began to travel in groups. Chronically clumsy unicorns were still deadly if you were caught unawares, and she couldn't count on tie-dyed bait hanging around to save her butt.

She needed a plan.

She had one. It wasn't sane, but little was in this crazy world.

So she hid in the same narrow alley as before, only this time she held a lasso.

Summers on her uncle's ranch were about to pay off as she waited for one of the pack to wander between its herd and the alley. She spotted a sickly, lavender-colored hide when one creature ventured close. It sniffed the remains she'd laid out as bait--they liked their brains fresh—then bent over to lick the carcass.

She exited the alley, swinging the lasso, while its back was to her. The beast was too engrossed in its meal to notice the sound but bolted when the thick rope wound about its neck. It jerked Maggie off her feet, yet she recovered quickly enough to mount the loathsome thing. It whinnied and bucked wildly, but she clutched its mane fiercely and pressed her body against it. The smell of its putrefied skin, among other things, made this experience less than pleasant, but in its zombified state its attention soon returned to the corpse at its feet. It stomped on the head a few times, and then bent to nibble at the broken bits of skull. The brains oozed onto the ground, and it fed.

She sat up, retrieved a metal rod from her backpack, and extended it. She also unpacked some entrails which she tied to the end of the rod. When the creature had finished its meal, she held the rod with the intestines dangling out of the creature's reach. Zombie unicorns followed their stomachs, and the beast lurched forward, snapping vainly at the lure. She held it closer to his mouth to slow his motion, but farther away to speed up.

Rounding a corner, she came across the rest of the herd. She recognized it immediately from the vomit-colored rainbow of horns and hides. By extending the rod farther she drove the monstrosity forward. The sleek and glistening guts bounced and swayed, and the beast charged ahead. The other undead raised their heads only seconds before the ravenous creature mowed them down with the long, glittery point of its horn.

Only a few creatures on the edge of the group escaped.

Now that there was plenty of flesh on the ground, however tainted and mangled, she withdrew the lure so the animal's attention was once again drawn downward. It leaned down to feast.

Maggie couldn't quite bring herself to pat the animal on the back (sitting on the rotting flesh was disgusting enough) though she did manage to croak out, "Good horsey."

Indeed. She'd let the creature finish its meal before using the lure again. Then she could take out the rest of the hellish things before disposing of the last unicorn. That was one problem solved.

Now if only she could figure out how to get rid of the damn fairies.

Fairy-be-gone

Sparkle hovered outside the window to the old house, ear pressed against the pane of glass.

"I'm telling you, Martha, I'm getting rid of that hive first thing tomorrow. Henderson's has some pesticide that'll do the job. I'm sick of dealing with the damn fairies."

His wife hovered over the stove, stirring some bubbling liquid with a wooden spoon. Sparkle scowled, both at the conversation and the spoon. Luckily, it didn't seem inhabited.

"Do you have to kill them, Roy? Maybe it's just they're attracted to the wood from the door you replaced. You could maybe buy a different style or something, and they might leave on their own."

"Why should I spend good money when there's plenty of fresh wood nearby? No, hon, you got a kind heart, but that's just not sensible."

"I just don't want the poor little things to suffer," said the farmer's wife.

"Heck, you wouldn't care if you'd been bit by the little buggers," said the farmer, "But don't worry. I'm sure it's painless." He kissed his wife on the cheek. "No more stew for me, Martha. Just going to finish up some things in the basement and go to bed. Early day fumigating tomorrow."

His wife smiled, and the farmer left the room.

Sparkle returned to the barn.

"We must act quickly, your Highness," said the fairy. "The humans plan to annihilate our home tomorrow."

The fairy Queen pondered this, tiny chin resting in the cup of her hand as she frowned in concentration.

Her small throne sparkled and shone within the center of the hornet-like hive. "We'd assumed the humans would think we lived in the nearby trees. This makes matters more serious indeed if they've grown impervious to our camouflage spells."

"But what of the poison? We may flee, but surely if he sprays that in here…" Sparkle gestured to the wooden rafters, then the barn in general.

The Queen's face softened. "Not to worry, my lovely minion. Tonight we shall make our move, and she will be safe. We may even manage to save our own home."

Sparkle relaxed, though she wasn't sure how they could save the hive itself. The magic of the hive wasn't powerful enough to protect it, and the entire fairy court combined couldn't move it by themselves. Nevertheless, she awaited her orders. Once given, Sparkle left to complete her mission.

The fairy Queen was known throughout the woods for her cleverness. Surely she would save them all.

Sparkle returned later with the news that both humans had gone to bed. The fairies posted a watch, and they got to work. From the topmost rafters they flew down to the small storage closet where the farmer kept his chemicals. Combining their efforts, they pulled the covers off cans of paint remover. Soon paint brushes hovered, dipped, and flew to the farm's newly replaced door.

They worked by the light of the full moon.

The fairies concentrated their combined magical effort on moving the brushes back and forth over the door's newly painted surface. When one side was completed covered, they sprayed the hose across its surface. Then rags removed any remaining red paint.

When the door had been wiped clean of every ounce of paint, the wood began to shimmer and shift form. Soon, the grains formed into the image of a young girl who gained depth as she stepped out of the wooden boards. She held her nose.

"Thanks, guys," she said, stepping outside the barn and removing her hand to breathe deeply of the night air. "But did you have to use something with so many fumes? It's almost as bad as the paint."

The fairy Queen laughed and said, "Almost, except that it isn't trapping you. You're free now, so stop complaining!" The other fairies tittered their agreement.

The dryad looked to the forest. "Do you think my sisters might welcome me when their homes are already full?"

"Perhaps," answered the Queen. "But now that you are free, we have a more pressing matter. The farmer that imprisoned you plans to destroy our home as well. Will you help?"

"Of course!" answered the dryad. "But what can I do? I'd offer you shelter…except I'm homeless now."

The Queen nodded. "I know, but I think I know something that will help us both." She explained her plan to the dryad, whose face lit up. Their combined magic just might be enough.

The next morning found the farmer standing near a suspicious red puddle in front of his new door, freshly stripped of paint. He scratched his head, frowning and muttering to himself. "What the…? Damn fairies. Malicious little creatures…" He squinted at the rafters, then climbed the ladder to the second level to check out the hive.

It was gone.

Well, whatever happened, at least it saved him the cost of a can of Fairy-be-gone.

The dryad knelt before the fairy Queen in the newly relocated hive.

"I accept your fealty, my loyal new subject. The services you've rendered this hive have been invaluable. Rise, Chloe. I dub thee 'fairy-kind.'"

The dryad rose and was instantly surrounded by her new sisters. She might not have had the wings, but she now fit into the small hive perfectly.

"What will your dryad sisters think?" asked Sparkle.

Chloe smiled, "They'll think I found the perfect home. Besides, I can always visit. We're not that far."

Chloe waved to her dryad sisters through the farmer's attic window, and the trees waved in return.

Pest Control

Luckily, Katie Kuttler found the stray fairy before her father did.

He kept an industrial size can of Fairy-be-gone next to the comfortable, threadbare recliner in the family room. Sometimes, while watching tv in the evenings, the little pests would sneak in, attracted to the flickering light of the boob tube. Mr. Kuttler would reach down beside the chair for his secret weapon, ready the sprayer, take careful aim, and (once clear of the glowing screen) he would spray the holy hell out of them, laughing as they floundered to their deaths.

Katie, a gentle soul with a tender heart, was always upset by these encounters but dared not voice her dissent. An avid reader, she couldn't help thinking of all the wishes and treasure lost to her father's dislike of these harmless innocents. As the room would fill with acrid-smelling fog, each sparkling victim resembled a shower of glitter as they fell to the stained carpet below. It was enough to make the girl weep. Such lost beauty and opportunity.

However, when she saw the glistening trail in the bathroom sink, she thought quickly. Grabbing the minivac, she sucked up the precious flickering fellow, snuck past her snoring dad, and quietly opened the household door to freedom. Once in the great outdoors of her front yard, she put her face up against the vac's clear plastic container and watched the tiny shimmering creature shout, jump up and down, and give her an incandescent finger. She grinned impishly. She'd let him go eventually, but there was no point in wasting an opportunity for free wishes from her adorable little captive, was there?

She grinned wider and returned one of the ruder gestures.

Cat Russell

Looking Glass

The woman chuckled as Lady clawed at the clear window. Pressing her nose against the glass, the dog whimpered, her breath forming small moist ovals of condensation against the pane. Beneath the small table, Princess Puggles whined for a different reason; her frail back legs, unable to support her ample frame, left her woefully floor-bound. Uncertain what marvels she was missing, she sat, firm but miserable, in the knowledge she was missing them. Meanwhile, her sister continued to follow the blowing leaf with the same fascination of a quest seeker in the presence of the Holy Grail. Earlier, she had seen a squirrel climb a tree and--delight of delights!--an elderly jogger wheezing across the busy street that ran athwart their house; both dogs occupied the dwelling along with their beneficently tolerant feline "sister" and a human. The woman shook her head again, wondering to herself at the insignificant things canines carried on about.

Winnie-cat shared this sentiment, perched peacefully on the windowsill, serene in her superiority.

Even the human, who had marginally better sight and intelligence than the feline's four-legged companions, failed to notice what was truly important. Winnie-cat eyed the sparkling pest pressing through the glass from a fourth spatial direction. Which was ana, and which was kata? She could never remember. She swiped sharp nails at the tiny beast, but it only continued to wave at her with aggravating friendliness. She batted at the creature again, but the glass continued to foil her best efforts to harm. Exasperating little creep.

The woman snickered. Doubtless at something in her large book of pictures, because Winnie-cat knew no human would dare mock a higher being such as herself.

Meanwhile, Crinkle-puff smiled widely, her shimmering wings beat a joyful tune as she waved. The ghost behind the human finally returned her greeting with a hearty thumbs-up gesture, before its ethereal form leaned once more over the female's shoulder.

Evidently the spirit found the bound papers entertaining as well. When it grazed against the corporeal creature, the woman huffed and smacked the back of her neck in irritation. "Damn, a fly must have gotten in."

In an adjacent room, a lone fly sat on the edge of the kitchen trash can, enjoying a free buffet of fragrant and sweet-smelling refuse. Undistracted and undisturbed, it enjoyed a perfect meal in peace.

Cliffhanger

George Griffith, affable and lovable nice guy, stood at the cliff's edge, hands raised high in the air. He was accompanied by his loving wife of twenty years, their next door neighbor, Bob, and the neighbor's annoying dog and cat. They mirrored George's stance to the best of their ability. Bob, however, was only able to comply with one upraised arm—as the other cradled a goldfish bowl. Inside the bowl, however, his betta fish (who was also named Bob) hovered in the tank's cloudy waters, his long floating fins in an attitude that suggested that he held his fins up in lieu of hands. The dog and cat merely lifted their heads.

"Now, jump." Mary Sue motioned with the revolver's long nose toward the cliff's edge.

George tipped slightly to view the depth of the proposed descent, then seemed to think better of it and edged slightly away. His companions did the same, mirroring his movements half a beat behind his own. The collars of the cat and the tiny dark pug made little tinkling sounds when they moved. Wet Bob leaned further away in his small glass prison. You may think it's impossible for a fish to lean, but I assure you, with determination, anything is possible.

"Uhhhh…no," said George, shaking his head from side to side.

His companions shook their heads from side to side. The little bells on the collars tinkled. Wet Bob swished in his tank.

It was annoying.

"Go on now," Mary Sue said, motioning the characters toward their imminent doom. "Jump."

George shook his head again, and his companions followed suit. They looked to George as their spokesperson. "What's my motivation?" he asked.

Mary Sue rolled her eyes, slowly inhaled, and silently counted to five before answering.

"Motivation? Are you serious?" She looked at the gun, then back at George.

George gave a quick, nervous laugh before answering. "Well…yeah. I mean, if we are going to jump off a cliff…*en masse,* I assume?"

Mary Sue nodded, and he continued, "If we are going to jump *en masse* off this very steep and scary cliff to certain death, wouldn't we need some pretty powerful motivation?"

"I'm holding a fucking *gun* on you," Mary Sue answered through gritted teeth. "*That's* your fucking motivation, asshole."

"But is it? Is it really?" George's voice had taken on the condescending tone of someone reasoning with an idiot, rather than a man bargaining for his own life and the lives of others. "Because from where I'm standing, I don't see how diving off a cliff is better than being shot." Just at that moment, an updraft from the unseen depths blew his hat dramatically from his head, whistling mournfully as if to emphasize the point. The other characters on the ledge followed the Fedora's progress with their eyes, heads turning as the wind whipped the accessory over the edge, until it was lost from sight. "See what I mean?" said George.

Mary Sue sighed and sat down on a conveniently placed boulder, careful to keep the revolver's barrel aimed at her intended victims. "Crap, crap, *crap,*" she muttered, then added an extra *crap* just to emphasize her point. "I was afraid this was going to happen."

"What?" asked George. Taking a tentative step toward her, his movements were mirrored half a beat later by his companions. When Mary Sue made no additional threats, they took a few more steps. "What was going to happen?"

"That the characters take control of the story," she moaned. "I mean, sometimes that makes my job really easy, you know? But others, like now, I have to worry about proper motivation, backstory, did I give enough foreshadowing. I mean, I *should* be able to just throw you all off a cliff if I want to, right?" She turned pleading eyes on her wayward creations.

"Well, maybe you just haven't come up with the right scenario yet?" said George, affable and lovable nice guy. He wanted to help her, even though she wanted to off him and everyone he cared about. That need to please at any cost was hardwired into him; it was one of the things that really didn't work about his character. She hated that.

"What better motivation could there be but a gun aimed at you and your loved ones?" Mary Sue was intrigued by his line of thought, despite herself. Well, because of herself, seeing how all her characters were just different manifestations of her own thoughts, but let's not quibble.

"Maybe…hmmm," George mumbled to himself, then brightened. "Maybe my wife was cheating on me with Bob!" He grinned. His wife looked horrified, but he continued. "Yeah, and I'm so distraught that I force them all off the cliff, then jump myself!" By this time, he had made his hatless way to her side and gave her a friendly pat on the back.

Mary Sue put her head in her hands. "No, same problem, right? You would just shoot them. How is a cliff dive better than being shot?"

"Because I don't need to worry about disposing of the bodies?" ventured George.

"He could threaten to shoot me in the groin!" volunteered Bob the neighbor (not Bob the fish). "That would be pretty horrific!" He looked pleased.

"Shut up, Bob. You're just a side character," answered Mary Sue. "I didn't even intend for you to have any lines."

Bob deflated, but George carried on. "No, he has a point. Some ways of dying are better than others, right? Painful versus painless, heroic versus cowardly, that sort of thing?"

Bob nodded his head in agreement, but Mary Sue glared at him before turning on George again. "Yes, but that *is* the point. I've just always wanted to throw my characters off a cliff when I'm sick of them, alright? Call it a writer's sadistic fantasy. I make no apologies for that."

"You're sick of us?" said George. Being threatened with different types of death had been off-putting, but that *really* hurt. "Why?"

"*Why?!*" countered Mary Sue, incredulity dripping from her lips like venom. "Because you are *annoying*, alright? Your character is flawed, and you say things like *en masse*. What real person says such a douchey thing? The characters I surrounded you with in the story are just window dressing, not fully developed people—which is why I have them mostly just react to you, George. Maybe I'm just a lazy writer, but it's easier to have them follow the main character around rather than come up with full personalities for each and every one. It's a short story, so is it even worth the trouble? And the animals! Holy frakking *hell*, what was I thinking with the animals? Half the time I forget they are there, so why'd I include them in the first place?"

"Maybe humor? You were being quirky," said George, unrealistically helpful, as well as affable and lovable as ever. Half a beat later, his supporting staff nodded agreement—including his wife, the dog, the cat, and the Bobs.

"They don't advance the story," she replied.

"What's the story about? " asked George.

"Me throwing you off a cliff."

"Why?"

"Because I'm sick of writing about you."

"Well…damn," said George. He swished his foot in the red dirt at the cliff's edge. The other characters did the same, except Wet Bob—who swished in his tank.

"What about the gun?" He pointed to the gun pointed at himself. "That's interesting, right? Imminent danger, all that…you could describe what it looks like, the long silver barrel coated in dust, the way *Chekhov* is engraved in elegant script along the side, the way you pulled it dramatically from the mantel to point it at us—"

"What mantel? There's just rocks here and a huge fucking drop."

"You're the writer, right? Couldn't you just *say* there's a mantel?"

"It's like I'm talking to myself."

"You are, remember? We are all just different manifestations of your own-"

"Shut up."

"-thoughts, but let's not quibble."

"You are missing the point." She glared. She sighed. She hung her head in frustration. She found many ways to express herself without actually moving from the spot, adding additional dialogue, or forwarding the plot in any significant way.

"Can't you just stop writing about us?" asked George, and his supporting cast…know what? You get the idea.

"No, it doesn't work like that," she answered. "The story needs to be resolved in a believable and consistent way."

"But how is throwing us off a cliff believable?"

"You see my problem."

"Well, for one thing you aren't *throwing* us off a cliff."

"Because you won't listen."

"No, not to criticize, but I mean, you are trying to make us jump—which isn't the same as *throwing* us off."

Mary Sue brightened. "You know, you're right. I don't know why I didn't think of that."

"Technically you did," said Bob the neighbor (not Bob the fish), "seeing how we are just different incarnations of your own thoughts-"

"Shut up, Bob," said Mary Sue, and she shot him. "I don't want to lose my train of thought, and I told you, you weren't supposed to have lines."

"-but…but…," sputtered Bob as the life drained from his body, "but…let's not…quibble."

George looked at her in astonishment. So did his surviving supporting cast. Bob the fish flopped helplessly on the ground, where Bob the neighbor had dropped the now empty tank when he was shot. Both Bob's burbled. It wasn't pretty.

"So…," mused Mary Sue, nudging both Bobs over the cliff with one steel toed boot, "if I just shoot you first, I can throw you over the cliff myself. Then I don't need to worry about your motivation."

"Nudge, not throw," corrected George.

She shot him. "And thanks for helping me establish *my* motivation." In quick succession she dispatched his supporting cast: the unnamed wife who resembled her own nosy neighbor, the dog that resembled the stray that tried to bite her every time she went out her own front door, and the cat that resembled the one that kept her up till three every morning with deafening feline orgies.

She set the gun back on the mantel that was mysteriously present in this deserted location. Then she bent down and shoved each one of her deceased creations off the cliff, whistling a joyful tune all the while.

Close enough, she thought.

Cat Russell

Femme Fatale

The man, exhausted from a full morning bent over the keyboard, grabbed the paperback from the shelf and plopped onto the sofa. Lying back, he opened the pages, prepared to surrender himself to the world another author had created. He read joyfully for the first hour or so, but with increasing wariness as time wore on. One of the main characters looked disturbingly familiar.

"Elizabeth?" the man wondered.

"It's Eliza now," she replied. The crisp black text coalesced into the shapely form of the novel's femme fatale.

"What are you doing here? In a murder mystery of all places. Aren't you classier than that?"

The woman, now fully formed, stepped out from between the lines. She knocked some letters out of her way with the sharp heel of her shoe and sat down. Her newsprint crisp skirt swayed as she kicked her legs back and forth. She regarded him through coal black eyes before answering. "Class has nothing to do with *where* you are. It's who you are and how you wear it." She brushed a stray 'w' from her skirt.

"How could you… What are you doing here?" the man asked, scratching his scalp. His face flushed with righteous indignation.

"I left you, Roy."

The man's features fell. "You left me? How could you…?"

"Oh, don't bother to look so surprised. You haven't looked at me in months." Her skirt billowed as she swung her legs with casual rhythm.

Roy got up and started pacing before the couch. "I had to put it down!" he said. "The story was driving me crazy. I couldn't see where the plot was going…"

The woman looked defiant but said nothing.

"Sometimes you need to put a draft down until you work out the plot problems. If you're short on ideas, you need to give yourself a break, let the well fill back up so you can draw on it again."

A smile creased the corners of her face like folded origami. "That's true," she said. "But you never came back."

"I meant to!" he cried. His pace quickened. "But life got in the way. There's so much to do…" He stopped, looking lost in the small living area. "I can't believe you left me for another author."

"I'd had enough, Roy. We were going nowhere fast. I wanted to live and see what possibilities life held for me." She pulled out a long tipped cigarette from the folds of her skirt and lit up, depositing the match on the table beside her.

"Aren't you made of paper?" the man asked, his gaze fixed upon the ashen end of the cigarette she held.

"I'm made of dreams, Roy." she said, blowing out a stream of cool blue smoke. "That's why I left you. You never realized."

Cat Russell

Capital Crimes

What is the meaning of this?

You are here, *Mister E*, due to the nature of certain letters that have come into our possession.

I've told you thugs before, my friend B is innocent! Since when is it a crime to say you don't like war? Who does?! Only madmen and—

I do not refer to your friend's anti-war sentiments, though that shall surely be investigated.

Stop shuffling those goddamn papers, and look at me! I don't understand. Why are you even reading the mail when—

Now, *you* are the madman, *Mister E*! An enemy may send coded messages, and even newspaper columns may be employed to—

No, no, no! I mean, why read *our* mail? We're just ambulance drivers, and B's only crime is hating all the blood and death we're exposed to in the service of "peace."

Aha! This "peace" you refer to is an example of exactly the sort of thing we are concerned about.

What? I don't…what?

The scare quotes you used when you referred to peace, which is the end goal of this military operation.

It's no secret that saying war in the service of peace is an oxymoron!

No, *Mister E*, I am not referring to your attitude but rather your punctuation.

My punctuation! What on earth does that have to do with anything?

Have you noticed, *Mister E*, how you have used punctuation and capitalization throughout our conversation? Even the questionable use of scare quotes? I have.

Well?

That is something notably absent in your published works of poetry, even to the extent of not capitalizing your own name.

…

Now, *Mister E*—or should I say *mister e?* what do you have to say for yourself?

I'm a writer! We expand the use of language; poetry often breaks the rules of prose—with the exception of prose poetry, and—

To the extent that you even lowercase your own name?

Hey! You used lowercase as a verb, and that's—

That is not the point, *mister e*. Do not *dare* change the subject! Who are you working for?

No one! My poetry isn't code for the enemy, I swear! I'm not working for the enemy!

And your idiosyncratic style? Besides the occasional odd usage of brackets and parentheses, your methodology makes no sense.

Hey, *watch it*! Art is in the eye of the beholder!

Eye and ear, apparently. Your excessive use of exclamation marks during our little talk is giving me almost as much of a headache as your printed works.

It's a stressful situation! I resent that.

You are meant to.

How can you accuse me of anything when you just ended a sentence with a preposition?

It was correct usage, and you are in no position to do anything other than answer my questions.

Listen, can you at least untie these ropes? I'm beginning to chafe.

No.

No?

No. Not until you explain.

That wasn't a proper sentence! There was no—*ouch!!!*

I see you are beginning to slip and reveal your true nature, *mister e.* Three exclamation points?

Dialogue is different.

How do you expect us to believe you are an author with so little vanity that you eschew capitalizing your own name? You must be getting paid a great deal, *mister e*, to go that far.

I swear to you, I am not a spy!

Spy? Who said anything, *anything,* about spying? Admit it. You are a saboteur.

If you don't think I'm a spy, then what am I sabotaging?

I ask the questions, *mister e*!

Ow! I swear to you, I'm not working for anyone! All I did was experiment with punctuation and grammar! Since when is that a crime?

Crime? You are not under arrest.

But the ropes, the cuffs…?

They are merely details to ensure your cooperation.

…

Who do you work for?

Wait, you don't work for the military?

Military, *mister e*? You wish. I work for a much more important organization.

Who? Dear gods, who could that be?

Let's just say certain union officials are unhappy with the turn the language has taken recently. The editorial costs alone are enough to put a significant dent in their annual budget—a fact which does not please them. So, once again, who do you work for? The CIA?

You just said it wasn't a spy thing!

Don't play dumber than you already are. The CIA in this context is obviously the Committee for Interrobang Adaptation! Is it them? A rival editorial group? The Typographers' Guild? Who? Confess.

if you could loosen these ropes and get me some water for my throat i would appreciate it all those exclamation marks really did a number on me

…

seriously

…

i will tell you everything for the right price

Stop smiling like that, *mister e*. It is giving me the creeps.

thanks for the water friend

You are evil.

Parts of Speech: The Untold Story

Housework could be a dangerous thing, especially in this house. That thought crossed her mind more than once as she performed her daily duties. She picked up another carelessly thrown interjection, cutting herself sharply on the word. It wasn't unusual. Perhaps she should wear protective gloves.

Cleaning her husband's office was especially dangerous. He'd often, in fits of rage, hurl expletives at the computer. The screen hadn't broken yet—most of the obscenities bounced harmlessly off to lay in wait for Sally on cleaning day. More than once she'd felt them lodge in her bare feet.

She made the best of it, extracting the sharp edges from her flesh to keep for later. She wrapped an especially descriptive epitaph in some tissue paper before placing it in her pocket along with other colorful phrases. She knew just what to do with them.

Her chores completed, she sat at the table and carefully spread her treasures before her. She enjoyed the feel of the sun on her neck as she worked, pulling her hair aside to catch more of the warmth that seeped through the window. The light spilled over her shoulders, shining on a rainbow of words.

She sighed. Way too many obscenities in the last batch. Not that she was a prude, but when overused they lost their punch. She sorted her harvest into the correct boxes—organized by category, sharpness, or turn of phrase. The commas and dashes she kept in a drawer with her paperclips.

She didn't know why her hands were shaking.

Recalling her friend, Michelle, Sally reflected on the similarity of their hobbies. Michelle scrapbooked with her friends, laying out their collected photos and decorations to assemble stunning family chronicles. Sally created a collage of words.

She grabbed some glue, grabbed a conjunction, and started a fresh page.

Super-Powered

Cranston Little was a towering beast of a man whose size belied his name. He stood in his cramped kitchen, huddled over the stove, stirring tomato soup with a small silver spoon. He noticed the cockroach skirting the salt he had poured around the stove's circumference and cringed. How else could he deter the insects that sought to feed upon his provisions? He had no wish to hurt them; all creatures had a right to live. But what else could he do?

The helplessness of his situation overwhelmed him, and he bent the spoon in half before he caught himself. Enough. He turned the stove off, hoping the insect would have enough sense to avoid the heat, and poured his soup into a bowl. Sitting at his kitchen table, he was finally able to stretch his legs and lift his head without hitting the ceiling. He needed to think. Whatever he considered, his situation was untenable. Every time he turned on the news, he was plagued with disasters he could have relieved, people he should have rescued, charities he might sponsor if he was ever able to leave the confines of his tiny apartment. Yet, how could he leave? If he walked outside, he might hurt someone, another creature, another human—though he barely felt human himself. If he shook someone's hand, he might break it. If he rescued someone from a burning building with the power of flight, they might have a heart attack from the shock. How could he live with the guilt?

He contemplated the number etched in marker on his refrigerator door. The antidote to villainy had finally been found; he was living proof. But if the conscience of the person matched their powers, what fresh torment would the most powerful man in the world endure?

Paralyzed by guilt and indecision, he huddled in his self-inflicted prison and ate soup.

53

Ronald spent most of his life trapped in the business world, placing a small noose around his neck each day and laboring under the lash of his inferiors. That was until the knowledge of his impending death liberated him from his humdrum existence.

Most people wouldn't consider the balding, pot-bellied, middle-aged man to be much of a threat. Until he'd glimpsed his inevitable doom, he wouldn't have considered himself much of anything. He had no family, no children, and no prospects except his looming fortieth birthday.

However, the gift of his single premonition changed everything. Once he'd glimpsed the end of his life's path, he was as upset as anyone else would be. Childhood dreams that he hadn't thought of in years suddenly seemed incredibly precious and unattainable. He only had thirteen years left.

When the ticking of the clock sounds like the footsteps of doom, thirteen years is all too brief. After a lifetime of mediocrity, he thought himself incapable of breaking his self-imposed mold. He lacked the funds to travel the world. He lacked the charisma and intellect needed to charm his way to the top of the business world. He would never live at the top of a Hawaiian volcano. He would never even live past his fifty-third birthday.

Yet, didn't age also hold promise? His time was limited, but it was also a *certainty*. Just as nothing could prevent his death, nothing could hasten it. He was indestructible. He wasn't a risk taker by nature, but for the next thirteen years death held no sway over him. Rather than a death sentence, it was an emancipation.

With this in mind, he realized the one childhood dream within his reach. He became a superhero. With iron-on numbers, blank t-shirts, and surprisingly comfortable tights, he created a costume to wear beneath his work clothes. He started wearing more comfortable shoes to work and carrying a few 'accessories' in his briefcase. With his new persona hidden neatly beneath his worn suit, he could transform in an instant into the dreaded Number 53, the Middle-Aged Marvel, Defender of the Innocent, Bane of Evildoers.

He used his invulnerability for the first time during his morning commute. He'd noticed a woman being followed into an alley by a shady looking character. The man pulled something out of his pocket as he followed the nervous woman. No one else seemed to notice.

Ronald looked around. Not a phone booth to be had. Damn cell phones! He'd just have to do with his mask. He walked into the alley and slipped it on quickly. He could hear voices.

"I told you, Dan, that's all I have! I can't give you anything else. Now, it's over. Please, let me go."

"Listen, doll, I think you've got something else I want, and I intend to get it."

'Doll?' Didn't that slang go out with speakeasies and guys named 'Bub?' Ronald thought.

He heard the woman gasp. "Get your hands off me!" A sharp slap echoed in the alley.

By now Ronald, shrouded in darkness, stood behind the thug. He feigned bravado. Stepping forward, he boomed in the deepest voice he could muster, "*YOU HEARD THE LADY. LET HER GO.*"

The man knocked the woman down and turned, his incredulity writ large. The woman lay sobbing quietly behind him. "Who the hell are you?" His jaw dropped as he took in Ronald's mask, business suit, balding pate, and unimpressive physique.

"I'm '53!'" said Ronald. He thrust out his chest and pulled open his button down shirt to reveal the iron-on letters beneath. *Damn, there go my buttons,* he thought, as he heard them plop onto the wet ground. He'd really need to think up a better way to undress in these situations. Buttons weren't cost effective.

The man looked him up and down, then started laughing. "I didn't ask your age, moron! What are *you* going to do to stop me?" He pointed a gun at Ronald's chest and snickered. "Looks to me like your days are numbered."

Ronald dove at the man's feet just as he pulled the trigger. Both Ron and the weapon's recoil threw the thug off balance; the bullet aimed high, ricocheted off the wall, and caught the man in the shoulder. With a cry, he fell heavily, cracking his head on the pavement. He was out cold.

"My days *are* numbered," said Ronald proudly. He turned and offered his hand to the woman. She'd stopped crying, took his hand, and let him pull her to her feet. Despite her tear-stained face and swollen eyes, she was rather pretty.

"Just so you know, Miss," he added. "I'm not fifty-three years old. It's just my alias."

She smiled at him, and for the first time in his life he felt truly alive.

The Mad Scientist

The evil genius hunched over the paper, laughing maniacally, shoulders shaking. His eyes, wide and wild, stared unblinking at the schematic.

"Honey, Tommy's got the catalog you were looking for!" shouted a woman from the adjoining room. She pulled a blowtorch from her white lab coat to prepare dinner.

"Damn it," said the boy's father. He'd better retrieve the paper. Despite his exclamation, he couldn't have been prouder. He set down the exploding mechanical mice he'd been working on and walked into his son's bedroom. "Junior?"

The boy looked up. Wide-eyed innocence filled his blue eyes. "Dad! You'll never guess what Evils R' Us has this year. I could get…uh, *we* could get our very own Moon-Disruptor for only seven billion dollars!"

"Well, that depends. Have you been good this year?" asked the boy's father. He coughed into his thick gloves to hide his grin.

The boy laughed again, the sound emanating from deep in his chest. "Never! I've been absolutely terrifying. The kids in my secret society fear me like no other."

"Hmmm, I don't know." The man rubbed his chin stubble and frowned. "That Moon-Disruptor's pretty pricey. We may not be able to afford it."

The boy's face filled with rage, quickly replaced by an even more disturbing calm. "That's alright," he said. "Some of my classmates' fathers have access to the material I need. I could build one myself, if you get me some plutonium. Have you tried searching Ebay?"

"No, son, that hadn't occurred to me, but I'll give it a try. After all, you're worth it."

"And then I can, uh, *we* can rule the world!" The boy did the laugh again. The vocal coach was clearly paying off.

The boy's father glowed with pride. His son, rather than following in his footsteps, might even surpass his own distinguished career. Madness, ambition, visions of world domination? His son's future looked promising indeed.

Life is Hell

Her family was going to Hell, and there was nothing she could do about it.

The red block letters stood out as she read the notice threatening to turn off her electricity. The foreclosure was wreaking havoc on her nerves, her husband's benefits were running out, the medical bills were piling high, and the goddamned dog wouldn't stop eating the couch.

She went to check on Amanda. The girl lay sleeping in her crib, her forehead beaded with sweat in the sweltering room. Why the hell was it so hot in here? No breeze blew through the open window. She shooed a fly from her daughter's face. What would she do when the benefits ran out? How would her daughter get treatment?

Bending to plant a kiss on the girl's forehead, she felt a sudden warmth tug her from behind. She turned and gaped, the wall suddenly funneling back into a bright spinning vortex. Searing heat pulled her, the room's furniture falling toward the hole, dragging them to the edge. The mother screamed, clutching her unconscious daughter, and bolted for the open doorway. Clutching her child, she threw herself into the hall and fell panting against the wall.

From the floor outside, she watched the portal expand. Heat emanated from its depths; its light left its imprint on her retina when she looked away, the image seared into her brain. Soon, her husband bounded up the steps. When he saw the vision through the open doorway, he slammed the door shut and wound his family in his arms. "I didn't know this would happen!" he sobbed. "It's fine. I can reverse this. It'll be just fine," he said.

The mother had her doubts. Acts of God (or mad scientists, for that matter) were rarely covered by insurance policies, and their policy would expire at the end of the month.

It had been years since she'd assisted Ralph in his work, but minions were one luxury they couldn't afford under present circumstances. She donned her goggles, adjusted the straps on her leather apron, and soldered the final piece of the machine into place. This would work. Their home would be destroyed in a matter of hours if the portal expanded exponentially, but Ralph assured her this would work. It needed to work.

She could barely stand to look as they aimed the reversal-gun at the gaping hole that had once been the heart of their happy home. She thought of their daughter safely stowed at her grandma's house. At least the old bat was useful for something. The damn dog remained confined in a kennel downstairs, in deference to her mother-in-law's allergies.

Presently, what remained of the house hummed with the machine's vibrations. Electricity crackled. Sparks flew. She took cover behind the protective shield alongside her husband, gazing up at the hole that had once been the nursery. The gun went off. A sudden explosion of light and heat sent them reeling, despite the shield, into the wall beyond. She watched in horror as the portal engulfed the rest of the ceiling. She wondered how long the roof would hold. How much longer did they have?

Ralph stood beside her, the expanding circle of fire reflected in his goggles. His mouth gaped. He made no attempt to move, and she screamed, "It's getting worse!" yanking him from his reverie as woodwork fell around them. "Goddamn it, Ralph! It's getting worse!"

Her husband turned to reply, his face blackened by ash and sweat. They dodged falling debris, and she caught the fiery glint on his goggles once more. "I don't know what else to do," he sobbed.

She stopped and watched him run through the screaming remains of her former kitchen. Soot and debris rained around her, but none touched. "Screw it, Ralph. We tried it your way."

She raised her eyes to the portal and muttered

ancient words. Her voice rose until she was screaming above the din, pointing at the light beyond. A fierce growl emanated from its depths. Smiling, she turned, grabbed the small kennel, and hurled it into the flames. There was one horrific howl; then the portal sealed itself, and the house was engulfed in silence.

She grinned. She had really loved that couch. Besides, their insurance did cover fire damage.

Cat Russell

A Little Bit of Sugar

Grandma smelled.

She didn't smell like cookies or fresh baked bread, but rather a sour combination of old lady, body odor, and Ben-gay. Billy could barely stand to set foot inside the old woman's trailer, but his parents insisted that he do odd jobs for her as part of his weekly chores. He sat and watched Grandma Moira lower herself into the Lazy boy in the tiny living room. The wallpaper had long ago faded to the sepia of old photographs.

"So, how's your mom and dad?"

Billy shrugged. He preferred not to get into discussions with the old woman. She tended to wax nostalgic at the oddest things, and avoiding conversation meant he'd finish sooner. "What would you like me to do, Grandma?" He stood up. "Wash dishes? Vacuum?"

The old woman stared up at him with dark, moist eyes. The skin of her face sagged under the weight of eighty years, yet intelligence still lingered in the depths of those eyes.

"Not just yet, Billy," she said, nodding at the couch. "Why not sit and keep an old woman company?"

Billy looked uncertain, but she insisted. Just for a few minutes.

He sat.

"I know you've probably got better things to do, but—"

"Grandma, I—"

"Now, now," she said. "Don't bother denying it. You're young, and it's perfectly natural that you'd want to spend time with other kids your age, not hanging out with an old woman." She looked at the floor.

Billy squirmed, sinking further into the plush, faded fabric of the couch.

"I'm sorry. I was just thinking of Mr. Tinkles," said Grandma Moira. "He hasn't been by in several days. You haven't seen him, have you?"

"No," said Billy, struggling to lift himself from the cushions partially swallowing him.

"That's too bad," said Grandma. "I thought maybe you might have seen him on the way here."

"Why ask me?" said Bobby. "I just came over to help."

"Well, of course you did," said Grandma, in her most soothing tone. "You're a good boy. Why else would you spend all this time with me?"

Because my parents make me, thought Billy, but he bit his tongue.

"Well," said Grandma, slapping her hands on her lap and hoisting herself out of the bulky chair. "You might as well get started on those dishes, and then you can go play with your friends."

Billy almost leaped off of the couch, except the suction from the cushions prevented it.

"You might as well have this," said Grandma Moira, offering him a rose-colored candy dish, "so you can throw it in with the other dishes."

The boy reached for the last piece of candy, but hesitated.

"Oh, go on," said Grandma Moira. "It's just a little bit of sugar."

The boy grabbed the candy—a small, rainbow-colored pebble—and tossed it in his mouth. It dissolved instantly.

Grandma's eyes hardened, two bright specks of coal in a face like fading paper. She pushed the boy back onto the couch, and he fell as limp as a ragdoll. "It's your own fault, you know," she said.

Billy's eyes remained fixed upon the terrifying figure that towered before him.

"I didn't want to resort to this, Billy, but you left me little choice."

His eyes widened.

"What really happened to Mr. Tinkles?"

The boy felt his mouth open, the words pouring out before he could stop them. "I ran him over Tuesday with the riding lawnmower."

Grandma Moira pursed her lips, considering. "Was it quick?"

"No." The word was out before Billy knew he was speaking.

She squeezed her eyes shut and leaned heavily on her cane, its gnarled wood supporting her weight. "Poor Mr. Tinkles," she murmured. "You were the best familiar I've ever had."

Billy's jaw slackened.

The old woman slumped once again into the overstuffed chair, contemplating her worn slippers. After a few minutes, she seemed to remember the boy's presence.

"Oh, yes," she said, directing another piercing stare at the boy. "Worried I cast a spell on you, aren't you, boy?"

Billy cringed, digging himself further into the sofa cushions.

The old woman cackled. "Don't worry, boy. I did no such thing."

Billy wanted to run, but his strength had already fled.

"I drugged you instead," said the old woman, getting up and retrieving the empty candy dish. "Witches dabble with herbs anyway," she droned on, picking bits of trash off the table. "You might say pharmacology is an interest of mine." She hobbled over to the garbage can and threw away the trash. "Though, the candy coating was a nice touch."

Billy struggled to extricate himself from the cushions, but they held him firmly. He would not escape.

"No, boy. You'll find yourself extremely open to suggestion for the next few hours," said Grandma Moira. She stretched, cracking the muscles in her back. "Which is why I'm calling your parents, and you'll confess to them what you did to my cat." She snatched the receiver from the cradle of the old-fashioned phone.

Billy sagged, and the old woman cackled again. "To my kind, boy, spells are prayers." She fixed him with another hard stare. "And I wouldn't waste my prayers on you."

Cat Russell

The Story of the Dandelion

When the world was young and the sky was old, the sun and wind became one. As he sailed across the heavens, she caressed his face with soft wisps of cloud, his golden beams piercing their billowy white layers. His rays caught the dust floating through her breezes. The first dandelion was born of this union, blessed with the bright face of her father as she blossomed from his warm touch. She returned to mother wind upon her death, but even then her seeds bore new life. Thus the eternal cycle began, sanctifying the earth and bringing joy to those fortunate enough to gaze upon a living field of gold.

Mangrove

Her roots reached down through the water into the dark, soft mud. It felt good to stretch and feel the coolness of the earth in the clinging tendrils that shot from her body. Though she enjoyed the company of the water's other animals—the long, lean birds that would search for food between her roots, the shelled creatures that used her for shelter—more than all, she loved the sleek rocky lizard that preyed on smaller living things. Perhaps it was his cratered body that appealed to her, a rock that waited with large golden eyes. She was earth, and he was stone.

"He'll never return your love," said the soft creature with the hard shell. "He can only have happiness with his own kind."

But the tree stretched her roots farther yet into the flowing water, offering more in the hope of greater return. But the craggy beast visited, neither more nor less, as he searched the cool water for his next meal or mate. Sometimes he waited in the shadow of her branches.

Her sisters crowded together along the shoreline, their roots mingling as they whispered to each other. They pulled away from her, though they themselves harbored similar creatures within their sheltered roots. None of them loved though, like she loved the dark brooding predator. His bellows sent shivers through her as her roots vibrated in the water.

Soon the lonely call of a water bird disturbed the stillness, and she remembered her loneliness. His company did not alleviate her solitude; it amplified it. It accentuated her inability to connect to him and to others of her kind. Her sister's presence did not console her.

The moon shone through her branches, dying them silver with its touch as she cast dark shadows on the water. The lizard took shelter in her presence, and she realized that the moonlight had changed him too.

It changed the water, her sister trees, even the distant hills. How could she have been so blind?

Penetrated and penetrating, she breathed the air that blew through her branches and transformed it into oxygen, giving life to many creatures—including herself. The wind slowed as it rustled her leaves, carrying the sound far away into the evening stillness. All occurred beneath the lovely sky of this world, the celestial orb spinning slowly through space and time, giving shape to the universe.

How could she be alone? She was one with them all, as the drop was one with the river.

She stretched her roots down through the water into the dark, soft mud.

Advice to a Young Girl Traveling in the Enchanted Forest

Now, dear, here's some advice before you leave the tall tower today.

Make careful note of your surroundings as you go so you don't get lost. And for heaven's sake, don't fall for the ol' gingerbread house trick! Oldest trick in the book.

And if you come upon a cabin in the woods, avoid it at all costs. Might look like a cozy vacation spot, but it's a *nasty* place.

Now, while you're out, stay on the path! If you come across any wolves or talking pigs, just be polite and move along. You don't want to mix with *that* sort. Oh, I know what you're going to say, but the wolves really aren't that bad. Just don't wear red; it drives them nuts.

If you get tired or hungry, you could go see that nice Rumpelstiltskin fella'. Sweet guy, he's raising some kids he rescued from terrible parents. Really! Is it any wonder Social Services has to be so careful, what with all the abusive or neglectful parents in this kingdom? Those kings and queens can be nasty! Always willing to make a deal with an evil witch or worse…

Oh, and did I mention the fairies? If you come across one, be on your best behavior, Missy. You don't want to end up like that prince that got turned into a monster. And don't believe that all beasts are princes either! Believe me, princes can be cruel but monsters generally have the sharper teeth.

Speaking of meals, if you meet anyone in the woods that offers you some food, DON'T TAKE FOOD FROM STRANGERS. I'll tell you about that foolish Snow White girl another time, when you aren't running late. Let's just say what she ate didn't agree with her.

Cat Russell

Now, button your coat, dear.

Listen, evil witches generally don't hang out in this neck of the woods, but we can't be too careful, can we? Anyway, you sure you want to meet up with this prince fellow? Alright, but we must keep up appearances until you know he isn't a disguised troll or a Belieber or something. Camouflage and secrecy are the best way to stay safe. Out the window you go, just take these shears and cut off the leftover hair once you get on the ground.

Don’t worry about the cleanup, dear. I’ll take the leftover hair and make an enchanted quilt or something. No, it’s not as creepy as it sounds.

Oh, and don't forget to be back before Midnight. That *never* works out well.

Snow White Retold

From within the crystal coffin, the fair maiden arose with the kiss of her beloved Prince. Vlad had been her intended before the Queen had broken their engagement and betrayed her; she'd charged the huntsman with bringing back her heart in a wooden box. Fortunately the weak minded were easily led, and he returned with the heart of a deer instead. Her animal minions had guided her to the house of the seven little men.

That day the ravens removed every last vestige of garlic from the premises while other creatures prepared a place for her. When the dwarves returned from their daily toil in the mines, they were seemingly enchanted by her cold white beauty and blood red lips. That evening, she spun her tale of forced exile by her wicked stepmother. With tears in her eyes, she begged them to shelter her.

She sought to win them over with a song. They readily agreed to let her stay if she promised to do the housework and—more importantly—stop singing. Both conditions met, all parties were satisfied. The men had been without a decent maid for months, ever since the Goldi-locks girl had cleaned their house out when she had… well, cleaned their house out. Still they stayed up late with the young princess, exchanging stories and not singing.

The next morning the seven bleary-eyed men left to toil in the mines once more. Before they marched away, they made her promise not to talk to strangers, especially old women bearing apples. As her eyes followed their progress into the woods, the princess—who had never worked a day in her life—resolved to spend the day waiting for her prince to save her from a dreary existence as a common maid.

No sooner had they turned a corner in the path when an old woman approached the cottage and knocked on the door. The princess peeped through a crack, but the hag elbowed her way inside. "Excuse me, young lady," she said, "but I'm a poor woman with many grandchildren to feed. Would you like to buy an apricot? Pomegranate? Perhaps a kumquat?"

The princess was stunned. "Kumquat? Isn't that indigenous to…where is this orchard anyway?"

"Oh, that is not important," said the old woman. "But I need to sell something in order to feed my grandchildren."

"Why not just give them the fruit?"

"Why not just…? Um, well…there's taxes, you see. Death and taxes, can't escape those, can you? And overhead costs, rent, cow dung isn't cheap these days either…"

"Alright already! If I buy something, will you leave?"

The crone's smile revealed broken, crooked teeth. From the saleswoman's basket, the princess chose an apple—partly because its color appealed to her but mostly to annoy the dwarves. She planned to feed the little men to the prince later anyway as a wedding present.

"Enjoy the fruit, my dear. It's my best season yet!"

The princess nodded and waited for the woman to leave. "Why aren't you leaving?"

"Just making sure you're satisfied, my dear. I may be poor, but I'm a responsible businesswoman."

Too bad the Prince didn't like older women, mused the Princess. The old biddy annoyed her and might otherwise make a nice snack. She rolled her eyes, sighed, raised the apple to her lips…

And collapsed.

When the dwarves returned from work, they found the princess sleeping inside a crystal coffin. "What took you so long?" asked the Queen.

"Well, some of the material components of your spells are harder to get than others," said Splotchy.

"You're lucky we had that much crystal on hand when we spoke earlier."

"It couldn't be helped," said the beautiful Queen. "Displaying the girl that way is the surest trap we can lay for Vlad. He's already turned many of my subjects, and to be brutally honest the garlic stench around the castle's beginning to get to me. Whew!" She held her nose.

Once they'd lugged the crystal coffin to a conspicuously open space, they hid behind a tree and waited for sunset. From the mountain caves beyond the forest, the prince flew to his betrothed, folded his leathery wings, and resumed humanoid form. Lifting the heavy lid, he bent over the slumbering princess and woke her to the life of the undead.

From within the crystal coffin, the fair maiden arose from the kiss of her beloved Prince. Their grins, filled with death (and on the Prince's part a little gristle), revealed sharp incisors. "Oh, my Vlad! How I've longed for your return."

"So have we!" cried the seven dwarves in unison, stepping out from the cover of the woods. The Queen held a cross, paralyzing the pair, while the dwarves rushed upon the duo with wooden stakes. Within moments, all that remained were two piles of dust mixed with clothing of questionable taste.

"So, you'll sign the contract now?" asked Burpy.

"Of course," said the Queen. "A deal's a deal. You helped me protect my subjects. Can't be Queen without subjects, now can I? So it's the least I can do. Besides, you guys are the best suppliers in the business."

"Aw, thanks, Mauve," said Burpy.

"That's Queen Mauve," corrected the Queen, glaring at the dwarf. Burpy hid behind Splotchy, who pushed him away.

The Queen's face cleared. "But let's not argue. My

cousin, Agatha, has a lovely house a little deeper in the forest. She's quite the baker. Her gingerbread is to die for! But I hear she's expanding into savory dishes. Tell me, boys, would you care to dine on a little roast Hansel?"

The dwarves, stout from their over-fondness of desserts, readily agreed, and they accompanied the Queen into the woods. Moonlighting as vampire hunters was, after all, hungry work.

Sleeping Beauty Retold

Long had the girl slept, cocooned within the thorny vines that embraced her castle. Long after the fairy curse had taken hold and forced upon her unnatural sleep, her parents and the other citizens of the kingdom had succumbed to the radiation that sickened humanity after the final World War. Toxic rain and poisoned water finished off those who had not died with the final deadly blast. Yet the princess Aurora slept on, immune by the unknown virtues of her curse.

The ship used its lasers to cut through the tangled vines, slicing a neat hole through the stones for its captain to enter. He stepped into the Earth's past, sheltered and preserved by the briars that had gripped the castle like a skeletal fist. The light from the device he held lit his face in the darkened halls as he watched its monitor for signs of life. It pinged softly, each ping grew louder and closer as he strode the stairs of the castle's tallest tower. By the time he reached the door of the princess, the noise had become a steady loud hum.

His large eyes widened as he pushed open the door to view the prone form of the girl, the last living woman on planet Earth. He pushed aside the dust covered canopy that surrounded her bed, gazing down at her beautiful features. Never had he seen a vision of such loveliness. Her long copper hair framed her face, like a Brill-o pad around a worn bar of soap. Saliva dripped from the corner of her open mouth, from which the odor of her last meal was still apparent—seasoned by age. When he leaned closer, he smelled cumin.

Remembering his research, he bent over the girl and brushed her hair aside, planting a soft kiss upon her hard and cracked lips. He stood back and watched her struggle to open eyes that had been caked shut by years of sleep. One eye opened. She rubbed the other, which opened as well. Bleary eyed, she gazed upon her rescuer. "Whazza…whozit?" she mumbled, shaking off the sleep of decades. To her hero, her voice was the melody of the past.

He pressed some buttons on his device. The machine pinged once more, then translated his words into electronic clipped tones that Aurora would understand. "Welcome back to wakefulness, Princess. I have sought your resting place for many years. This is a very important discovery."

The woman propped herself on elbows that popped audibly, then squinted into her benefactor's large black eyes. "Huh?" She strained to focus on his face. Skin the color of ripe avocado, eyes that blinked slightly less often than she liked, and a large, bulbous head as hairless as a cue ball. If she was still dreaming, she figured she might as well play along. "Who are you?" she managed. Aurora ran her tongue across teeth that hadn't been brushed in decades. She definitely needed a brush.

The little man pressed more buttons on the device. "My name is Zork, chief of Galactic History for Sector 42. You must accompany me to Zeta Prime where you will be questioned on Earth culture."

The woman swung her legs over the edge of the bed. She gingerly tested each one until she stood on them both. "Wait a minute," she said, reaching for a brush on the nightstand and attempting—without much success—to run it through her hair. "I read books, you know. I'm not going anywhere until I get my prince." She glared down at Zork. The little man was waist-high. "Rules are rules."

The little man's skin darkened to a deep forest green. He tapped the device. "Our civilization has evolved beyond the feudal system of more primitive sociopaths."

Aurora backed away and gripped her brush. Dream or not, this still *felt* real.

Zork checked his device, then tapped again. "Apologies. More primitive societies. There is, however, a Galactic President."

The woman relaxed her grip on the brush. In her mind's eye, solar systems did a slow waltz across galaxies which spun slow, lovely pirouettes. A thought struck her, shattering the image, and she blurted, "Beyond primitive so…so…so you don't rule any land?

The green creature looked at the ceiling for a moment, then tapped again. The electronic voice chirped, "I own half of sector 42, which includes this solar system as well as several others." He tapped, "This gives me exclusive historical excavation rights over said property. Is this sufficient to meet your requirements?"

Princess Aurora gazed down at her small saviour. Ruler of the whole freaking planet? A prince would be a step *down*. "Zork," she said, smiling sweetly through taco-stained teeth, "take me to your leader."

Hand in hand, the two stepped aboard the shining craft. The saucer flew into the starry void.

Cat Russell

Red Riding Hood Revised

If Grandma hadn't been so cheap, the whole mess could have been avoided. As things stood, Red was forced to hike through the woods carrying the heavy wooden basket. When she knocked on Granny's door, the growls from inside let her know exactly how bad the situation had become. In one swift blur she grabbed her gun, kicked in the door, and shot a silver bullet between the creature's eyes. Then she retrieved her surgical tools from the basket to perform an emergency gastrectomy.

A sheepish looking Granny emerged from the gruesome remains. "I know, I know," she said. "Next time I'll buy the wolfsbane *and* garlic. I just wanted to save a few pennies. I'm on a fixed income, you know."

Goldi-locks Part 2

The burglar glared at her jailers through the bars as the clock struck for the noonday meal. The policemen laughed and chatted, closing the door behind them, as the small girl struggled vainly in her handcuffs. With the final click of the lock, she spit the hairpin into her hands. She wasn't called 'Goldi-locks' for nothing.

The thought of the cops' faces when they returned to find her cell empty split her face into a malicious grin. With a deft movement the cuffs fell from her wrists and she grabbed them before they clattered to the ground. Years with Pops hadn't taught her manners, but picking locks came as easily to her as breathing.

As she glanced through the door's small window at the sleeping guard, she let her thoughts drift to the little fink that had exposed her. The world knew him as 'Baby Bear', but to her he was simply a rat. Surely she could think of worse things to do to him than eating his porridge. She swallowed the remnants of her conscience and headed for the door.

Cat Russell

Rumpelstiltskin

The Queen had but one bright spot in her life, and soon he would be gone forever.

As a young girl, her father had lied and bragged that she spun straw into gold. The greedy King had overheard his subject's drunken boast and imprisoned the girl with one command: "*Spin gold by morning or die.*" The Queen remembered how she had sat at the spindle and wept bitterly for the life she would never lead.

But then the creature, a little man of light and shadow, had appeared from nowhere—like a miracle. He seemed to pity her misfortune and offered to aid her in her need. How could she know how high his price would be? How could she choose to do anything but live?

The creature had spun the straw throughout that night so many years ago. His fingers flew, and soon the cold gleam of gold replaced the musty straw. The air tasted of metal. Before the sun rose again, the little man had disappeared without a word.

The Queen still remembered the King's delight with the night's work. Instead of taking her life, the cruel King had taken her hand in marriage: an act he soon repented when he found she had no gift for gold. Over the years, he made her suffer for wasting his life on a common maid.

And yet, after years of pain, she had given birth to the child, the bright shining sun around which her life revolved. The King almost forgave her.

But then the little man returned.

The Queen wept bitterly as the gnarled little man snatched the squalling bundle from her arms. She turned her face into her husband's chest, heaving great sobs at the loss of her beloved child.

"In three days' time," said the little man, his eyes filling with tears, "if you guess my name, I will return the child to you."

The silent King wrapped his wife in his arms. His eyes shot daggers at the dwarfish figure scurrying into the shadows. All too soon, the child's screams died with distance.

Once home, the little man removed his hood and hushed the child in his arms. "There, there," he cooed, producing a bright golden rattle. The babe's eyes lit up, and soon the creature's cottage reverberated with the sound of childish laughter. The creature treated the child well, fed him sweets and all nature of good things for three days. Then he returned to the queen.

"Do you know my name?" he asked. His name was a secret, shrouded in mystery. He did not fear her answer.

But then, he did not know of her spies. He did not know how they had heard him sing the child to sleep, sing his own name (in the security of his home) as he promised to care for the child as his very own.

Now the moment for truth had come.

The Queen glanced at the harsh face of her husband, again at the little man cradling her child in his arms, and answered, "No." She washed the infant's face with her tears as she kissed him one last time.

The little man turned and walked from the castle, humming a tune for the child. The Queen returned to her gilded prison, secure in the knowledge that at least her child was free.

Cat Russell

The Witch and the Frog

Blasphemous and profane hymns filled the room as the hag threw ingredients into the boiling cauldron. "Eye of newt and toe of dog," she sang. From a rotting shelf, she grabbed a dish and threw its contents into the pot. Foul odors rose with the steam as she babbled arcane phrases mixed with snatches of old tunes.

On the windowsill of the stone tower, a frog croaked, watching the proceedings with interest.

"Snakeskin next," she called. The small serpent wriggled as she tossed it into the bubbling liquid. She cast a backward glance at her amphibian observer. "Then a witch's clog." She reached down, pulled off her right shoe, and tossed that into the concoction.

She shot a brief look at the frog as she stirred the loathsome brew. From a hook on the wall, she removed a ladle. She dipped it into the pot and blew away the steam before drinking.

Thunder roared. Lightning flashed. Arching her back, she cackled in triumph before orange flames consumed her body in an explosion of heat and light. When the smoke cleared, another small frog sat in her place.

She hopped over to the windowsill and asked, "*Now* will you kiss me?"

Fame

Rudolph ran as fast as his four legs would carry him. He had run out of fairy dust over a remote forest, and unfortunately it was deer season.

The celebrity found it hard to blend in with his shiny nose. In fact, it was damn near impossible. His schnoz glowed like a blinking beacon, one the hunting party was only too glad to follow. He heard a voice, not far off, call, "I see him over here, boys!"

Damnation, but they were close!

Rudolph searched the area. Could he pull the ol' mud over the nose trick again? No, who was he fooling? He might as well admit his time was up. He kept running though, out of habit rather than hope. What else could he do?

Then, just ahead, salvation! A homely cottage in the near distance, invitingly close, with a fence and—thank Santa!—a bright red sign that said, "No Hunters Allowed." Above the door he could make out the words, "Happy Home Animal Shelter."

A lovely woman with scarlet hair beckoned him inside the fence. "Quick, dear, before they find you! You'll be safe here!"

The calls close behind him, Rudolph ran inside the gate. He wanted to thank the woman for her hospitality, but he didn't know what to say. She turned to him, smiling broadly. "You don't need to thank me, dear," she said. "You must be hungry after running so hard."

Why could he no longer hear the hunters? He glanced at the cottage. Now that the adrenaline was wearing off, he noticed more details: the candy-colored shutters, the aromatic smell of gingerbread.

He turned a questioning eye upon the woman, whose smile turned feral.

The gate shut behind him.

Dammit.

Three Little Construction Workers

Henry had no skeletons in his closet, no matter what people said.

Construction was in his family's blood, and Henry, along with his brothers Howard and Horace, had been born to build houses. Rather than combine their talents, however, the three brothers decided to go their separate ways, each one starting his own construction company.

Was it really Henry's fault that his brothers couldn't handle the business? Competition had never been their strong suit, but Henry seemed blessed by the gods with good luck. At least when it came to business. Henry had never shared his brothers' knack for making friends, and most people avoided him when possible.

Unfortunately, his brothers did not share in his good fortune. If only they had agreed to merge their companies and talents! But they refused to see reason, and eventually—despite repeated bribe attempts—Howard and Horace were run out of the construction business for repeated safety violations by the indescribably ferocious building inspector, Wolfgang Howitzer. Miserable after their failed business ventures, they soon disappeared, never to be seen again.

Meanwhile, Henry, who passed all safety inspections regarding the construction of his buildings, enjoyed an unprecedented prosperity that lasted well into his old age. His one close friend, Wolfgang, had never cared about money so much as a good meal, and disposing of Henry's competition had been a wickedly pleasant endeavor for them both. The Inspector enjoyed several delicious, morally and ethically reprehensible meals, and Henry enjoyed an easy, profitable retirement.

He had no skeletons in his closet, having stowed them both safely beneath the cement foundation of his most successful apartment building.

OPENING LINES

Cat Russell

All Happy Families

All happy families are alike; each unhappy family is unhappy in its own way.

What a load of rubbish.

Georgia was willing to bet that most "happy" families were not happy, but merely appeared so to outside observers. At least, this was true for her own family. Sure, she was gifted with looks, wealth, and plenteous magical abilities, but all that meant was you had more to worry about losing. Were her friends really interested in her or simply what she could do for them? It was like the lottery. Once you won, you had more friends than you could count, but were they really friends?

In a way, it was worse, because she had no basis upon which to judge. At least lottery winners could reasonably suspect that strangers suddenly turned chums might be posers. But the lottery of life had been in her favor since birth. Her father was a powerful wizard, her mother a wealthy socialite and self-funded superhero. None of that hidden identity nonsense from them; they didn't believe in it. But oh, how Georgia wished they did.

She fiddled with the chemistry set her best friend, Montana, had given her for her sixteenth birthday. Another unfortunately-famous child; her parents were equally well-known, though in a different way. She felt, with a reasonable amount of certainty, at least Montana could be trusted. Well, with one glaring exception.

"So, when do you think your dad is getting out of super-prison?" asked Georgia, mixing another potion in the transparent beaker.

"I don't know," Montana fumed. "It's bad enough that he hasn't been there for *most* of my birthdays, but you think he'd at least want to be there for my sweet sixteen!"

"Well, it's not for another month," said Georgia,

consulting her father's secret potion book, the one she'd snagged from the crystal cave below their mansion. He may have been a master of the mystical arts, but he was crap at keeping secrets—from her, at least. With a few magical phrases she'd easily enchanted her way into his "secret" workshop. She dropped a bit of purple dust into the beaker, a miniature rainbow briefly poofed above the glass container, and a tiny dove the size of a pencil-eraser flew out of its liquid contents before the colored prism dissolved back into the glass. "And he's been on good behavior, right? Maybe the parole committee will cut him some slack."

"Hmmm," said Montana, observing the tiny display thoughtfully. "I think it needs more cinnamon." She leaned back and grabbed a bottle from the spice rack they had borrowed from the kitchen. "But maybe you're right. There haven't been any incidents, other than that toad thing…which hardly counts." She added the cinnamon to the potion, but nothing happened.

"And that was just a small incident, right?" said Georgia cheerfully. "I mean, he didn't really hurt the guy." She shook the beaker and frowned at its contents.

"Well, he threatened to dissect him, but nothing ever came of it." Montana took the spell book from her friend, tracing the spine with her finger as her eyes skimmed the book's contents.

"So he changed him back?" asked Georgia, putting down the glass container.

"Nope," mused Montana, glancing up from the page before her. "He said the guy was more agreeable that way. Besides, there's worse things that can happen then getting turned into a toad."

"Hey!" said Georgia brightly, "I've got an idea. We haven't included nearly enough Ingredient X in this. Just a sec, I think my mom left some in her lab." Quickly, the girl exited the room, leaving Montana to brood over her father's fate. Only two weeks left until her sweet sixteen. Why did the bastard have to knock over that billionaire's cruise ship? So what if it would have funded his research. She wanted him *with* her. She was his daughter. She deserved to have her father around, even if he was a brilliant, insane, amoral scientist.

"Got it!" Georgia plopped back down on the plush carpet and added Ingredient X to the beaker. When purple foam began to overflow the glass container, she joined hands with her best friend, and they began chanting.

Soon, the foam dissolved into a small rainbow-colored unicorn with brightly sparkling wings, but the girls continued chanting. Montana smiled. She'd never been much of a girly-girl, but if that was what her friend wanted to give her for her birthday… "Congratulations," she said. "It's a…horned Pegasus?"

Georgia grinned broadly. "You mean, it's an escape plan." She thought directions to the tiny creature. The glittering horn drew a large oval on the container's side, which burned away like acid, then delicately stepped outside and laid down in front of Montana. "He can help your father get out for your birthday," she said. "Do you think I'd let my one and only friend be sad on her special day?"

Montana gasped in feigned astonishment, even forgiving her friend for calling her birthday her "special day"—what was she, five? She hugged her tightly. "And he'd have to go back afterwards?"

"Well, of course," answered Georgia. "We can't have him running around unsupervised. It'd be far too dangerous." She didn't have the heart to tell her friend that the tiny little monster would dissolve shortly after it helped her father escape. For a girl with dastardly parents, Montana was far too kind-hearted.

"Of course," said Montana, contemplating how to hide her father without her friend catching on. She would never send her father back to prison. However, with her burgeoning superpowers, she felt confident she could control him. Implanting the escape plan in Georgia's mind had been easy enough, and—after all—he was far older than her friend.

Montana grinned, contemplating all the while how she could use her developing mind control powers to help make the world a better place. Hell, at the rate her abilities were progressing, she might even be able to use them to make *everyone* happy.

All it would take was a little concentration.

*"All happy families are alike; each unhappy family is unhappy in its own way." —opening line of Anna Karenina by Leo Tolstoy

Cat Russell

Ishmael

"Call me Ishmael again, and I'll break your face," I warned the middle-school moron towering over me. Honestly, I was pleasantly surprised the idiot had made the literary reference. Considering his schoolyard vocabulary and his frequently vacant expression, I thought he'd taken one too many blows to the head during his tenure as the pack's alpha male.

You might think the top dog in this schoolyard would be an adult, but in my neighborhood you'd be dead wrong. Literally. His strength, agility, and ability to make almost anything into a weapon had helped him survive, but I'd had outrun scarier things than him in my single decade of life. Still, it was usually safer to travel in groups. Loners were picked off quickly.

Buster's cronies hung on his every word, shoulders hunched, tensed for the coming assault. "You think you're so tough. 'Lot o'good your books will do you when we feed you to the dead."

I *knew* it had been a mistake carrying my copy of *Moby Dick* around with me, but when I'd found the book during a recent supply run I hadn't been able to resist. Was it my fault Buster's parents were eaten before they taught him to read?

Taking a stand had been poor judgement, but I'd always been small, and old habits died as hard as the dead themselves. I glanced at the putrid mob outside the fence, decaying fingers curled around its wire, hungry for my flesh. Then I focused on my human enemies *inside* the fence.

Sure, *Moby Dick* was famous enough that even this lumbering turd was familiar with it. People still told stories, after all, though reading and writing were quickly becoming lost arts. A thought suddenly struck me.

Screwing up my courage, I walked over and punched him in the nose. "My name is Stu." His henchmen gasped and retreated as one.

Buster stood his ground—gods, he was built like a mountain!—but he wiped blood from his nose and there was murder in his eyes. "Oh, you'll be *stew* alright, when I'm done with ya’!" Gripping my shirt, he pulled me so close I inhaled the stink of his breath.

Nose to nose, I seized my opportunity, whispered my offer. "I'll teach you to read," I said, voice low. "No one has to know. Just don't kill me." He paused, fist drawn back for the punch. How could he take advantage of my offer without backing off in front of the others?

Now was the time to save his face as well as my ass.

I held my hands up to ward off the blow. Cowardice was more necessary at the moment than bravado. "Please don't hurt me! I'm sorry, I'm sorry, I'm sorry!" A beating was coming, as inevitable as the fact that the dead always rose to come after the living. I could take a beating, then remain in the relative safety of the pack.

He threw me to the ground, smiling; his right hook found my nose, which soon was bleeding more profusely than his had been. He enjoyed each punch, raining blows upon my prostrate form, my cries music to his ears. As stupid as he was, he knew enough to not damage me too badly; I couldn’t teach him if I died. Meanwhile the dead shook the wire barrier, incensed by the violence and the scent of fresh blood.

Ours would be a mutually beneficial arrangement. Protecting me would ensure his future literacy. He bore me no love, that much was evident, but when the day inevitably came when I was of no further use, I had one final card up my sleeve.

Speed.

They say knowledge is power. I knew the bulk that gave him strength also slowed him down. When the day eventually came when he turned on me, I would see it coming. I would outdistance him, leave him for the dead, and escape while they feasted on his ample frame.

Moby Dick wasn't the only book I'd ever read, after all.

*"Call me Ishmael."—opening line of Moby Dick by Herman Melville

AN OPTIMIST'S JOURNAL OF THE END OF DAYS AND OTHER STORIES

2014

It was a bright cold day in April, and the clocks were striking thirteen. Dave hit mute on his alarm and kept walking, collar turned up against the Spring chill. Each year the world became colder, the skies darker with the satellites floating above the Earth in their never-ending quest for "safety through vigilance." Today's weather was overcast, the clouds obscuring the metal monstrosities that dominated the skies. Most people never looked up.

The neighborhood had gone down in the past few years, the once burgeoning community was now littered with abandoned houses that lined the street like trashcans on pickup day. Paint peeled, a few of the windows had been broken. Despite cheerful news reports of the growing economy, people continued to lose their jobs and storefronts stood empty in the heart of downtown. Still, the government ensured that even the poor had cell phones.

He entered his apartment and noted the camera on his computer screen, the eye that never shut. Government hacks into civilian technology had already been revealed, but most people had already forgotten the initial scandals, distracted by the latest fad, the hottest celebrities, the more recent scandals. Why worry about cameras on their cell phones when gas was over three bucks per gallon?

He brought up the bookstore app and considered purchasing another novel. George Orwell had long been one of his favorite authors, but yet he hesitated. He looked at the selection on his phone's small screen. If *1984* was considered seditious, why were stores allowed to sell it at all? Why did libraries still carry the text, schools still stock Orwell's science-fiction among the classics? Did he honestly believe it was science fact, details skewed but prophetic nonetheless? He thought about not buying the ebook. He could get it through a used bookstore, pay cash, keep it off the radar and avoid observance as well as convenience.

Cat Russell

He glanced across the street at the abandoned houses. His neighbors had been questioned, sure, but why had they left? Why did their homes stand forlorn and broken? It couldn't be economic downturn. The radio spat out new stats every day; the country was thriving. Yet, he wondered when it would be his turn to be questioned. Would it be a phone call summoning him to the authorities or men in black coats at his door?

No, all that was needed for the death of liberty wasn't an oppressive state but citizens too scared to exercise their rights. He chastised himself for reading too many dystopian novels, even as he hit the word 'buy' on the phone's touchscreen. He back-arrowed into his e-library and downloaded the newest purchase.

The phone rang. He stared at the caller I.D. Swallowing hard, he left his apartment, closing its door behind him.

*"It was a bright cold day in April, and the clocks were striking thirteen."—opening line of 1984 by George Orwell

They Say When

They say when trouble comes close ranks, and so the white people did. They pulled together, arms locked, expressions vacant, sinking into the snow on the side of the road as the grey rider approached. Nothing showed but their eyes, ebony coals burning against the stark alabaster of their skin, their white cloaks mimicking the color and texture of the snow.

Vaughn pulled up his silver steed. The animal smelled something, that much was plain. The grey rider had learned over his years on this strange new world to listen to the instincts of its lower lifeforms. He patted the animal's side, stroking the scales with something akin to affection—or what approximated affection for a man unfamiliar with the concept. "What is it, girl?" he thought, sensing the animal's bloodlust, her anticipation, her thrill at the proximity of prey.

In the snow, not two feet from the creature's feet, a dozen whites shivered from something other than the cold.

*"They say when trouble comes close ranks, and so the white people did."—opening line of Wide Sargasso Sea by Jean Rhys

Cat Russell

The Past is a Foreign Country

The past is a foreign country: they do things differently there, thought Brandon479 of Gamma colony, Mars. He knew looking into space was looking into the past, and though the Earth was only light-minutes away, he marveled at the sight: the lightshow, the swirling clouds of ash on the surface of their former home. What would the shockwave do to his home on Mars?

The Martian settlement had been established as a community for those outcast by the rest of humanity, a place of refuge for those who did not fit the molds society had created for them. While the elite and wealthy of Earth lived in towering citadels of gleaming silver, the politicians bickered in their ivory fortresses, and the lower classes served the whims of the higher, the outcasts on Mars tilled red soil using ancient instruments and experimented with new, exotic species of flora for consumption as well as beauty. Worlds apart, though only a planet-rise away.

The Martian, Klarg, nodded to his human companion, then pressed a flashing light. The green-skinned creature was grimly dissatisfied that the planet's force-field was necessary. Having taken too much time to lull the human puppets into submission, the Earth would no longer be a prize worth conquering. If only they hadn't destroyed themselves first, he felt quite sure the Earth humans would have made excellent slaves. The ones on this planet had seemed subservient enough.

*"The past is a foreign country: they do things differently there."—opening line of The Go-Between by L. P. Hartley

Far Out in the Backwaters

Far out in the uncharted backwaters of the unfashionable end of the Western Spiral arm of the Galaxy lies a small unregarded yellow sun…or at least, it would for just a bit longer. But everything ends eventually. Everything has a beginning, with its end already present at its inception, its termination born of its genesis. Life makes room for other life, degrading into its component particles, which in turn become something else. The same is true for all things, living or otherwise, though the sun really resented this.

It had been born, as so many other stars had, out of clouds of stellar dust brought together by mutual attraction, heating up and briefly fueling the worlds that revolved around it with the matter and means for the development of life and complexity. What, in turn, had that life ever given back? That's what the sun wanted to know.

Now that he was on his last legs or atoms, whatever—all the intelligent lifeforms that had visited or been born on the planets of his solar system had taken off. It seems they were too good for red giants; just because he made the planets uninhabitable, that was no excuse for rudeness. They flew from his system, propelled by ship, wings, fins, or combustible gases to take root in other systems around other stars. Fickle bastards.

So with a flash of helium, his shell collapsed, and no one marked it. He shed layers and layers into the vastness of space, but no one bothered to comment on his nakedness. He radiated his annoyance into the boundless unknown, but the heat was felt by nothing. Finally, out of energy, out of time, he took comfort in knowing that his death would start the process all over again. Life would eventually develop once again from his component parts—no matter how far away.

Then he'd show 'em.

*"Far out in the uncharted backwaters of the unfashionable end of the Western Spiral arm of the Galaxy lies a small unregarded yellow sun."—opening line of The Hitchhiker's Guide to the Galaxy by Douglas Adams

BEWARE OF GREEK GODS

Cat Russell

Who Mourns for the Minotaur?

My mother loved me, but how could she? I was the living, breathing embodiment of her shame: a beast born of bestiality. Whether my father lives or not, I don't know. I certainly never knew him. All I've known is this maze and—in the distant fog of memory—the tower. Our tower.

Why could not Daedalus have taken me too? He took the boy, and oh how I envy him. Not just his escape, but to have a father who loves him, to have everything that was denied me. What did I know of my mother's adultery? As for my father, I never knew him.

Not the one who *sired* me—to my mother's everlasting shame, nor the one that might have raised me (all unknowing of my real parentage) were it not for my resemblance to the divine bull that fathered me. If my sire was so beautiful, the gift of Poseidon that Minos refused to sacrifice, why am I considered so monstrous?

Or is it my resemblance to my mother?

What infant could earn such wrath? Why punish me for my mother's faithlessness? Still…in my dreams I remember her, a woman with sad eyes who cradled my infant form, stroked the fur behind my ears while singing sweet lullabies. Hers was the only kindness I've ever known.

In the tower we shared, we'd watch the landscapers, the mathematicians, the workers of clay and wood and mortar: all their work overseen by Daedelus, the supreme architect of my misery. She would smile mournfully as children ran and played at the worksite, weaving their way freely through growing corridors that would one day be my prison. I wonder now if they were my brothers and sisters. I wonder if she knew what awaited me or merely suspected, all while she told me stories of gods and men and of my grandfather Zeus wooing my grandmother in the form of another divine bull.

Why then did Zeus turn a deaf ear to my prayers?

Bulls, she told me, were beautiful: sleek and muscular, divinity of form. My beastly sire was nothing to be ashamed of, but a source of pride. Her shame was her own, her faithlessness to her husband, her broken marriage vow that led to our imprisonment was her fault alone.

I know her words were meant as comfort, but even as a child I couldn't help but suspect the fault partly belonged to her husband, Minos. Had he been less cruel, she may have been more faithful. He may not have struck her, but could someone who imprisons a child be anything but a monster?

My divinely created father is eternally absent. I do not know his fate.

After many years, young men and girls have come to my maze. Do they know the way out? Are they my half-brothers and -sisters, come to rescue me as Zeus rescued his siblings from the cruel bowels of Cronus? No, for with my every appearance, they run away in terror. Their faces speak truths their tongues do not. They are prisoners here, just as I am. They can never leave, just as I cannot.

But at least they have each other.

I miss my mother.

The other day one of the youths came at me with a long sharpened stick he must have made from the surrounding greenery. I ran, but he pursued until I was trapped. I reached to wrest away his weapon, to plead with him, to tell him if he would but be my friend I would show him how to feed on roots and sweet berries and survive. In the struggle, he pierced himself with his own lance. I screamed as he smeared my browned skin with his scarlet blood.

It's the first bloodshed I've ever known, though I caused it—all unknowing. Can Minos say the same?

The maze is open to the sky, and I can feel the sun's warmth, the cool breezes, hear the chattering of birds. If only the sounds of the lost youths were as sweet. I wonder what Daedelus and his son are doing now.

Perhaps, if I keep my ears tuned and eyes turned skyward, I will see them return for me.

Dream Guy

Susan gestured to a balding, middle-aged man standing in the cafe door. "Isn't that your boyfriend?"

Amanda saw him, then turned to stare at her cup. "He's not my boyfriend," she hissed.

Susan leaned over the table, her face inches from Amanda's. "Secret admirer then," she whispered.

Annoyed, she blew a strand of stray blond hair from her eyes. "Don't look," Amanda whispered.

Susan raised her eyebrows. "What do you want me to do? Hide behind a newspaper?"

Amanda watched the swirling steam in silence.

Passengers screamed and ran for a safety that didn't exist. The lifeboats were gone. Men, women, and children slid as the deck tilted 45 degrees. A screaming woman fell toward her, heels headed straight for her face. A split second before impact, Amanda felt herself tackled and hurled over the edge.

She flew over the water with her rescuer, too shocked to speak. They landed safely inside one of the lifeboats floating in the icy water. Even as she watched the cruise ship sink, she couldn't believe their luck.

She turned to thank her savior, but when he looked at her she completely lost her nerve. The large bushy eyebrow spanning his forehead made her cringe in fear, like a hairy monster about to go for her throat. She passed out.

Susan kicked Amanda under the table. "Snap out of it, stupid!" she whispered. "He's coming back."

Amanda sighed. She looked up as her homely savior approached. "Is this seat taken?" he asked.

"No, not at all." Amanda pushed the chair towards him. Susan shrugged and smiled, blue eyes sparkling. He blushed slightly and set down his paper and coffee.

"Oh, excuse me," he said, "I forgot my sugar." He went to the counter, leaving Amanda alone with her friend.

Susan still sat in her chair, except now she towered over Amanda. A glob of thick, vicious venom dripped from her fangs as she slurped lemon-strawberry milkshake from an oversized straw. Black and orange hairs sprouted from her enormous exoskeleton. One of her eight multi-jointed legs sprawled lazily against the window. She regarded Amanda with large, compound eyes.

Now, that's odd, thought Amanda. *Didn't she have coffee?*

"So, chicken, what are you going to do?" asked her monstrous friend. A couple of the black hairs fell into her drink, and she cursed loudly.

Amanda shook her head. "I just don't know. He seems…"

The spaceship shook. The planet was literally coming apart around them, but she couldn't get the damn engine to start. If they didn't make it off this rock soon, they'd be torn apart. "I could fix this!" she cried in frustration. "Doesn't anyone have a…" Someone handed her the part. She looked up, not entirely shocked to see the smiling, ugly face of her benefactor. She smiled, despite the ominous bushy eyebrow over his otherwise benevolent face. "Thanks, I…"

He gestured to the engine. She recovered, screwing the final piece in place. The rocket tore into space and safety. She would have been crushed, regardless, had it not been for the safety belt that he'd strapped around her. They looked back at the quickly receding fireworks. She found herself holding his hand and blushed. He'd just saved her life. Twice. Nevertheless, she firmly resolved to keep a pair of tweezers handy from now on.

Quiet, mild mannered, handy to have around. She didn't consider herself a shallow person, but that damn eyebrow turned her nerves to jelly.

Susan nudged her with a hairy, jointed leg. "Stop zoning out, girl. He's coming back."

On cue, the man pulled out a chair and sat down. A wry smile tugged the corners of his mouth. *So help me*, she thought, *he's almost…cute.*

He put out his hand. "You know, I've seen you around, but I've never properly introduced myself. Call me 'Morry'."

She shook his hand. "Morry? Oh, nice to meet you. What sort of name is that?"

His eyes glinted. "It's short for Morpheus."

"Oh." She looked at him and then her arachnid friend.

They both laughed. She felt like she should be annoyed but wasn't. "What's so funny?"

Morry nudged Susan, who stifled a few giggles. "Nothing," he said. "It's understandable you'd be confused."

"What?"

He smiled. "I just thought my name might have tipped you off." He grasped her palm, and images flooded her mind. The sinking ship, the exploding planet, pajamas sleeves flapping as he flew through the air.

"You're wearing pajamas."

"Yes," he said. "I know."

"In a coffee shop."

"Yes,…well, sort of."

"You're wearing pajamas in a coffee shop and I…you keep rescuing me."

He nodded.

"And I never found that strange until now."

"Don't forget about me!" chided Susan. Her giant fangs were slathered with pink foam.

"And my best friend turned into a giant spider which I didn't think was strange either, so…"

He smiled at her.

"I'm dreaming."

"Yes."

"Duh!" cried Susan happily.

"I don't get it. Why you? Are we…?"

He smiled. "You're dreaming. You've been dreaming for a very long time…ever since your accident."

Accident? She rubbed her temples with her fingers, struggling to remember. She could see the motorcycle, her helmet lying bloody in the ditch, and then white walls.

"So, Morry…I mean, Morpheus. You aren't real?"

"Oh, come on, girl. You're so close!" said Susan. Amanda wondered how intoxicated a giant spider could get from milkshakes.

She looked at Morpheus again. She remembered flying, lifeboats, holding hands and an exploding planet. She remembered hundreds of other encounters, times she hadn't recalled more than a few instants after they'd happened.

"But…Morpheus, Morry—sorry, but if you are *the* Morpheus…why don't you, uh…"

"Why do I look like this?" He smiled, and even with the unibrow he was *almost* handsome. "Well, I wanted you to love me for myself."

She was stunned. "Love you?" She didn't know what to say, but then another thought struck her. "You mean this isn't the way you look?" She hoped she didn't sound too eager.

"Well, I am a god, but…this is my natural appearance."

She tried to hide her disappointment.

He grasped her hands and asked, "So… do you think you could love me?"

She looked in his big brown eyes and saw kindness, generosity, and modesty.

"On one condition," she said. She pulled a hand away to give him something from her pocket.

He gazed at the small gold tweezers and laughed. Soon, she started giggling too, along with everyone in the cafe.

Above the din, Susan called, "Soy-lattes for the happy couple!"

Cat Russell

Tempting Fate

Clotho inhaled, enjoying the heady aroma of roasted beans and caffeine that permeated the small coffee shop. The temptation to step inside and grab a cup was irresistible. She didn't know if mortals could actually smell caffeine, but it gave the goddess a deep sense of satisfaction--almost like the burnt offerings humans used to make to the gods in the past. But not now. Now, if they burned her coffee? Well, she'd be pissed.

What's the worst that could happen?

A little chime sounded on the Fate's cell phone. In the old days, there had been an actual tiny bell that would appear and disappear, but she savored the advancements that came with the passage of time, just as she savored a good cup of joe. She also liked the little bell sound. Best of both worlds, really.

And why not? She wasn't trapped by linear time the way mortals were, but she enjoyed watching its passage from their perspective. She sipped her coffee, sighing with pleasure. The little bell chimed again.

What's the worst that could happen?

Long ago, she'd put a filter on the alert, only taking note of those "great ones" who tempted Fate with those fateful words. Great ones? Ha! Just another term for "more fun to mess with." As if politicians and celebrities held more sway over the tapestry of life than she and her sisters--or even wandering beggars in the right circumstances. Just pull the right thread, snip another, and whole swaths of cloth would unravel, only to be rewoven in the pattern of their choosing.

Even the gods themselves knew not to tempt Clotho and her sisters, for while they could be generous, they also found a challenge hard to resist.

What's the worst that could happen?

Let's see. Buddha and Christ had both been beggars

who changed the world for the better. Would she be that generous this time? She checked her notifications to see who had tempted…well, *challenged* her so often in the past few minutes. Upon seeing the name, she scowled and decided that perhaps *this* time, she and her sisters would not be kind.

She texted Atropos and Lachesis about this latest challenge. Their reply?

This will be FUN.

Clotho chuckled to herself. Two more mochaccinos suddenly appeared on the counter in front of the startled barista; the goddess grabbed the white Styrofoam cups, tucked her cell back into her earth-friendly tote, and headed out the (now) automatic doors.

Cat Russell

Lightning Rod Salesman

"What are you selling again?"

The man with the paunch sagging through his frayed sweater scratched his comb-over and contemplated the stranger on his doorstep. He watched the man remove his fedora, run fingers through his short-cropped blond hair, then replace his hat.

"Lightning rods," he said. He fidgeted with the worn leather satchel.

"That's what I thought you said," said Horace, his gaze pinning the younger man like a bug under glass. "You do know this is the twenty-first century, right?"

"Oh, yes," said the salesman, brightening. "I'm glad you brought that up, sir. You see, some of the world's great minds believed in the usefulness of lightning rods. Why, Benjamin Franklin invented one! Tesla improved on Franklin's design and—"

"Cut the crap, kid," said Horace, turning his gaze upon a falcon that flew through the deep blue sky. "Why do I need one? I'm not exactly living in a skyscraper now, am I?" He gestured to the decaying floorboards of the porch he now stood upon.

"Listen, sir," said the salesman. "I'm not just selling rods. I'm selling a lightning protection system. You see, the idea is to place these so—"

"Again, kid," said Horace, eyeing the clear azure beyond the salesman's head, "I don't really need them…uh, it."

The salesman's face fell, and the older man's expression softened. "It just seems like you don't know your market here. I mean, I'm in the middle of nowhere. I'm not living a life of luxury. What made you think you'd make a sale here?"

The young man sighed. "Listen," he said, blue eyes pleading. "Could you maybe just buy a couple? My old man, he…uh." His shoulders sagged. "I really need to make this sale."

Horace sighed, looked up into the heavens, then said, "Family problems, eh?" He rubbed his left eye. Its pupil never dilated, though the sun had retreated behind some clouds. "I know what that's like," he said, then blinked. "Tell you what, I have some money put aside. Hell, I'm old. What am I saving for, right?"

The salesman's face lit up. "You wont regret it!" he said, pulling a long metal bar from his satchel. "I'll even install it myself. Cash or check?"

"Oh, heck," mouthed Horace, fishing around in a clay jar inside the door. "Cash. A check just feels like an unpaid debt until it's cashed anyway." He handed the younger man a wad of bills.

"Thank you," said the salesman. "This'll make the old man so happy. My first sale!" He smiled, then sobered. "Don't worry. I'll install it for you right away."

"Ah, I have faith in you," said the older man. "You just take care of that, and I'm going inside to watch my soaps." He turned his back on the grinning salesman and let the door creak shut behind him.

"Faith," said the younger man. "If only more people had faith." His dusty traveling cloak melted into a sparkling white toga, his battered leather boots into golden sneakers that sprouted tiny golden wings. The fedora became a gilded helmet with matching wings. He looked at the roof, sighed, then rose into the air. "Father, don't you think this is a bit petty?"

Heat lightning flashed, followed by a faint rumbling. The god went about the business of installing the rods without grounding them. "I know you're competitive, but—"

Another flash, another rumble. "Fine, target practice," grumbled the god. "Have it your way." He sighed again. "I'm all for pranks, but this? Swindling an old man into making his house target practice? It's just…such a waste of my talents."

Rumble.

"Fine, I'll be home for ambrosia later." The golden youth picked up the leather satchel, slung it over his shoulder, and leapt from the roof.

From the second story of the farmhouse, Horus sipped his tea and watched the winged figure diminish, swallowed by distance. "I don't hold it against you, poor lad," he mused. "No one picks their family." He touched his eye again, then picked up the pamphlet from the table.

Zeus could play his prank while he was at the museum. The Egyptology exhibit promised to be even more popular than the Greek one, and he had tickets for opening night. He could repair his home when he got back.

Even for the god of a long dead religion, godhood had its perks.

The Dogcatcher

The man crept through the alley, the net behind his back gripped fiercely in one white-knuckled fist. From behind the metal dumpster, a dog peered with coal black eyes. Suspicion and curiosity clouded his features, but his ears pointed up and his head tilted to the side in the universal language of dogs. The young man approached, side-stepping broken glass and wads of chewing gum, bent low with agitation and concern.

"Hey, you bad boy. You got out, didn't you?" he called, his voice a whisper on the wind, comforting yet strong. "It's alright, boy. Just come here, and I'll take you home. No hard feelings, right?"

A second dog's head appeared behind the first, this one growling low, long strings of saliva dripping from his deadly maw. The man stopped in mid stride, one foot inches above the pavement. He held this position a moment, listening. From behind the dumpster, snoring could be heard. He sighed. Why couldn't they *all* be sleeping?

He snapped his fingers, and a bucket of fried chicken appeared on the pavement before the large metal bin. The snarling stopped, replaced by a short bark which woke the other head. The curious first head was already leaning forward to reach the bucket, frustrated with the other two for hindering his progress; the chicken lay just out of reach. Soon the complete dog emerged, all three of its heads diving for the food, growling and snipping at each other as they fought over legs and wings. Meanwhile, Hermes slipped the magical net over the entire dog and pulled it closed with one deft movement.

Cerberus thus entwined, the winged youth hefted the net over his shoulder and headed for the Underworld. Next time, he would plan his pranks on Hades with a little more care.

Cat Russell

A Time to Remember

The hunter stalked the high school dance like a panther stalked its prey.

Through the foliage, he peered at the festivities within. He brushed aside golden curls and watched the roiling sea of taffeta and tuxedos amid a riot of streamers and tinsel. A lone banner declared it was 'A Time to Remember.'

On the building's west side, social outcasts grouped together, casting furtive glances at the dance floor. Spiked punch did little to alleviate their anxiety. One awkward teen looked especially forlorn as the object of his desire crossed the makeshift stage to accept her crown.

Perfect.

Outside the gym, the camouflaged youth pulled a gleaming silver arrow from his backpack, fitted the deadly instrument into his bow, and waited. The crowned couple descended the stage and danced amid a wide circle of admirers. The King spun his partner westward, and the hunter loosed his arrow—into the heart of the unsuspecting girl. She stumbled, fell from her partner's grasp, and was caught by her most unlikely suitor.

Amazed, he pushed his horned-rims up the bridge of his nose and helped the girl to her feet. "You fell…"

She looked into his deep brown eyes and smiled. "Yes, I did."

Then the King pushed the outcast away, grasped the girl once again, and resumed the dance. It was too late. Eros's shaft had hit its mark.

The god slung his bow over his shoulder, zipped up his hoody, and smiled.

Naughty

The secrecy, the excitement of sneaking behind her husband's back, gave her a rush like nothing else—especially since she knew full well her lover could kick his ass in a New York minute. But what would be the point? He'd only be accused of picking on a cripple—no matter how resourceful that cripple might be. Besides, divorce was out of the question; Daddy wouldn't hear of it.

But when lover boy stripped off those fatigues and leather? *Yum*. She just couldn't help herself. She loved bad boys, and he'd been very naughty.

That evening, Hephaestus munched popcorn and mulled over suitable punishments as he watched the DVD of his wife's antics. *Oh, to Hades with it*, he thought. He'd had dalliances of his own. Besides, judging from the tape, the love of Ares was punishment enough.

Cat Russell

Creation

Hera could feel it coming again. This time she could feel herself fading into oblivion, instead of fighting a hopeless fight against the forces of destructive creation. She held her brother-husband's hand in her own, small comfort against the weakness that enveloped her, enveloped them all. For a time they had fought, with words and acts of grace and goodwill, fought to retain their places in humanity's heart, but no more. It was over.

It was over for them all. Humanity itself had ceased to exist, or at least had evolved to the point that the gods no longer resembled their worshippers at all. Where kings and queens, presidents and politicians, had once ruled the Earth, now the peoples of the planet had interbred with other species to the point that they would be unrecognizable to their own ancestors. And they thought gods had played games of fate by breeding with the mortals below! How was the Minotaur an abomination, but neo-humans were not? It made no sense, in Hera's mind.

And now, as the stars extinguished themselves in the big crunch of existence, even the neo-humans themselves were huddled together for their last bits of light and warmth before their own lives were blown out forever. The gods themselves were in the same place—spiritually, mentally, emotionally, and physically—for how could gods live without worshippers?

Nothingness extended for the briefest instant throughout the cosmos, the instant without time because time no longer existed; then everything exploded in a shower of creation, new forms emerged from the old, recast into new molds. From the destruction, everything began anew, everything was new, and time—with one small hiccup—started again, like a clock being wound and reset for a brand new day.

BARDLINGS: SHAKESPEARE WITH A TWIST

Cat Russell

The Willow (a la The Tragedy of Hamlet, Prince of Denmark)

The willow grew near the brook, and the girl had often climbed its branches in her youth to gaze into the cool clear water. Despite her father's prohibitions, she found her only solace there. The constraints of rank and privilege had always weighed heavily on her young shoulders: she often spoke to the tree and confided her deepest thoughts to its silent form.

When she grew older and her father died, she fled once more to the willow's embrace. She felt her father's presence there—scolding her even as she searched the waters for a peace she no longer possessed. The branch she perched upon broke, giving beneath her and falling into the crystal blue water.

She knew she should swim. Instead, she opened her arms wide, her tresses a golden halo, her dress spread like angel wings. The water caressed and carried her, and while it bore her up she sang snatches of old tunes. When the weight of her clothing pulled her down, the songs of her childhood ceased—along with dreams and guilt.

The tree, ever her friend, had provided her escape.

Puck's Surprise (a la A Midsummer Night's Dream)

Fairies were neither prudish nor temperate by nature, but when Puck's pranks graduated from tipping old ladies to strategically placing whoopee cushions, he crossed a line. Something needed to be done.

"But what?" asked Oberon. Puck had served as his wingman for years, so he wished to handle the situation delicately. Several compromising photos were at stake.

Titania suggested an intervention, though Oberon thought the idea unproductive.

"I agree," called a voice. "He'll think it's a joke, take it as a challenge, and be worse than ever."

"Who speaks?" called Titania.

A delicate fairy woman appeared out of the crowd and knelt before the thrones. "Buttercup, my liege."

"Well, do you have any better ideas?" said Oberon.

She grinned.

Later that afternoon, Oberon searched the woods.

"Puck! Robin Goodfellow!" called Oberon. He'd thrown dignity to the wind when he told Titania that he'd fetch Puck for the party, but he didn't dare disappoint her again. He'd never live it down.

A nearby bush moaned softly, and Oberon pushed aside some leaves. "Puck? What are you doing here? I've been calling for nearly ten minutes!"

The wayward fairy rubbed his temple and moaned again. "Sorry, my liege. If I had been conscious, I would never have dared keep you waiting. Do you have some aspirin?"

Oberon produced two small pink tablets. "I'm always prepared."

Puck sat up, scratched his hairy belly, and fished around on the ground for his beer cap. Fitting it to his scalp, he popped the pills and sipped from one of the cap's straws. "What do you need, sire? Having trouble with the Queen again?" He rose unsteadily. "You know, I could get Cobweb and Mustardseed for you. They make a mean—"

"Really, Robin, you've been around mortals too much! That's depraved, even for you, and—"

"—chocolate cake."

"What?"

"Oh…oh! You thought I meant—"

"No, of course I didn't—"

"Of course not. Not after last time, right?" Puck nudged the King and winked with one blackened eye.

After an uncomfortable silence, the King asked, "What happened to you?"

Rubbing his forehead, Puck said, "I really don't remember, sire. There was this party—"

"Of course," said Oberon.

"And all I… ah, I remember. Fraternities have no sense of humor no matter what they say."

"What did you do?" asked Oberon. "Make an ass out of yourself again?"

Puck grinned. "No, but I think I made one out of them!"

Oberon sighed. "Not the donkey head again. What is it with you and donkeys? That's the oldest joke in the book."

"Actually, pardon my liege, but you're thinking of *the chicken that crossed the road.*"

After another pause, Oberon continued. "Anyway, you need to come to your birthday party."

Puck perked up. "Party?"

"Oh, I know. You don't get enough parties, do you? But yes, and Titania won't let me cut the cake until you blow out the candles and—"

"Cake?" The color returned to his face. "Did Cobweb and Mustardseed make it?"

"I don't know. It's a cake: chocolate with—"

Puck took off towards the court. Thunder boomed. Puck returned, bowing low. "After you, sire."

"That's better," said Oberon. "Now, let's get some cake."

The crowd formed a wide circle around the large multilayered cake. Titania sat on her throne, resting her chin in her hand.

"Can I come out yet?" a muffled voice called.

"No, not yet. You know your cue!" snapped Titania.

"Yes, your Highness," said the cake.

Just then Oberon entered the hall, followed closely by Puck. Everyone quieted and knelt before the King. The Queen straightened up and offered her hand to Oberon, who kissed it before sitting beside her. With a small nod from the royal couple, the Fairy Court rose again.

Puck ran to the cake.

Everyone sang a tune roughly kin to 'Happy Birthday', and on the final line a scantily dressed fairy woman popped out of the cake. "Surprise!" she said. Puck pulled her out and kissed her passionately.

"This is going to be the best birthday ever," he said.

She guided a straw to his lips, so he could swig more beer.

The next morning, Puck awoke in the arms of the lovely Buttercup. He gave her a quick kiss on the forehead, licked some frosting from her hair, and patted her affectionately on the butt. He grabbed his boxers from a nearby twig and started to dress. "Thanks for a good time, but I gotta split."

Buttercup rolled over and regarded him through heavy lidded eyes. "Where do you think you're going?"

Puck tried vainly to put on a boot before realizing it wasn't his. "Oops. Sorry."

Buttercup sat up. "No, but you're going to be."

"Hey, relax, babe. It was an honest mistake."

"That's not what I meant," said Buttercup.

"Okay, whatever. Have you seen my shoe?"

"Look at your finger."

Puck looked carefully at his finger. "What? My shoe…?"

"No," breathed Buttercup. "Look."

Puck looked. A small silver band glinted in the morning sun. "What the…?"

"We're married."

That brought him up short. "Married? How much did I drink last night?"

Buttercup smirked. "Quite a bit, but that's not the best part."

Worried, Puck asked, "What's the best part?"

"The binding spell I put on your ring. You're bound to me for life. I know your tendency to stray, but from now on, wanderer…," she smiled again, "your ass is mine."

Puck mulled this over. He liked bad girls; maybe this would be fun.

"What do you think about open marriages?" he asked.

A wicked grin crossed her face. "I said you'd be obedient," she cooed. "Get rid of your whoopee cushions this instant!"

"Yes, Mistress."

Cat Russell

Pucked Up (a la A Midsummer Night's Dream)

Puck looked at the watch and pondered the nature of time.

It was almost as fickle as he was.

What marriage—or a good binding-spell brought on by too much drink and a serious lack of judgement—had bound together, time would tear asunder. At least it would if Puck had anything to do with it. Robin Goodfellow was not a fairy that would remain tied by one woman for long, no matter how fun bondage might be.

Belching loudly, he sat up, snapped his fingers and produced two ice-cold cans of his favorite fizzy intoxicant. Crumpling and tossing the empties, he re-loaded his beercap. He stood, scratched his hairy belly, and brooded over his newly acquired wife.

Buttercup lay frozen on the flowery bed, a beatific smile softening features that would otherwise have appeared harsh in the early morning light. No, who was he kidding? She always looked angelic, no matter how much spandex she was wearing. Still, if he was tied to her by the terms of her nefarious binding-spell until "the end of time," the obvious solution was to stop time, right?

Puck contemplated the charmed silver band that graced his finger. Buttercup was many things, but a fool was not one of them. In fact, he might even go so far as to say she was as shrewd and knavish as himself—a perfect match. So his solution seemed almost too easy. Was it another trap?

However, Robin Goodfellow was not known for his caution. Snagging the watch from the fairy king had been risky, but he knew his boss would be too busy "making up" with Titania to notice its absence. He removed the magically-binding wedding ring, then turned to face his lovely bride. He'd make the bitch pay, but there was no reason her punishment couldn't be fun for both of them. He pressed a button on the watch's side.

Time once more in motion, his blushing bride opened her eyes; her smile slowly widened as she took in his appearance.

"Hello, darling," she said. "Want to play?"

Cat Russell

All's Fair in War (a la A Midsummer Night's Dream)

The two maids had been inseparable since the cradle. Hermia's outgoing nature and natural charisma complemented her friend's shy and quiet personality, and Helena never begrudged her friend's popularity; she preferred the company of books to most of the addle-witted boys of Athens. But when her own fiancée' cast her away to chase after her lifelong friend—the gloves came off.

The abruptness of his change of heart shocked everyone. Throughout his courtship of Helena, Demetrius barely noticed her friend. In fact, during the Duke's engagement ball, he'd paid more attention to Hermia's father. The two men conversed the entire night.

Only days later, he asked the Professor for Hermia's hand in marriage. Surely some art swayed the motion of Demetrius's heart. Helena knew he wasn't so shallow as to be lured by the wealth and position of Hermia's family.

Still, she'd seen his eyes when he met Hermia's father. The Professor was an impressive figure. However, the way he favored Demetrius made her…uneasy.

All was fair in love and war, and Helena intended to win at any cost. But who was her rival? The fair Hermia or the Professor?

Cupid was a knavish lad.

Fortune's Fool (a la Romeo and Juliet)

Romeo had always had a way with the ladies, never taking no for an answer, no matter what question was asked…not that he usually bothered. His last girlfriend had become a nun to get away from him, but Rosaline's loss was Juliet's gain. He knew that. He knew he was a pretty boy. In fact, the chicks were fond of reminding him, often telling him "You're lucky you're so pretty." He would have preferred to be described as ruggedly handsome, but whatever worked, right?

And Juliet was *hot*. The fact that her parents were his family's mortal enemies made her dangerous too. *So* sexy. They'd sneak off to neck just around the corner from her hot-tempered cousin. She seemed to get off on pissing off her family. Hell, she'd even talked him into marrying her, knowing he'd do whatever it took to seal the deal. True, the danger wasn't just an aphrodisiac—that business with her cousin was unfortunate, and Mercutio…

Mercutio was entirely his fault.

Why did he insist on screwing around like that? If he'd just kept his hose on, his best friend would still be alive, Juliet would still be alive, and he wouldn't be banished and forced to live like a beggar outside Verona's walls.

But he thought he could at least partly make up for things. He'd already screwed up his life, he had no future, he was a wanted man, and with his new wife dead and a bounty on his head thanks to the Capulets, he'd never get laid again. At least not without paying a hefty fee, and how could he afford that now?

The poison in his pocket would take care of his problems. If he was going to go down, he'd rather be thought the devoted lover than a coward who couldn't face up to his crimes. But first, that dandy, Paris, was sniffing around Juliet's tomb. He'd be damned if he let another man near his wife. He'd already paid dearly to be with her; no one else would. He'd dispatch Paris with his blade before he drew his last breath.

Then Juliet would be his forever.

What Really Happened to Juliet? (a la Romeo and Juliet)

Juliet Capulet had always hated her name.

A rose by any other name would never smell as sweet if it had been fertilized with the crap her family inflicted on her. She was dying to escape, when the soft-brained Romeo offered to take her away from it all. Sure, he had the attention span of a spaniel, but he was easily as cute and trainable. She could land a new life and piss off her parents in the process. And according to the Friar, all she had to do was swallow a little sleeping potion.

What the hell? she thought, I've done worse. I've already slept with the enemy; I'm aiding my cousin's killer. How could things get any worse?

So she did the deed, took the drug, and slept the sleep of the seemingly dead for days.

The Friar, their secret conspirator, sent the boy a message telling him of the drug-induced sleep—a scam sure to fool both sets of parents. Unfortunately, Romeo never checked his mail. Instead, his friend informed him of her "death", which sent the simpleton running to his lover's tomb to kiss her frozen lips and take his own life.

Stupid kid.

The grieving parents interred his bones with that of his beloved, consoling themselves that at least the lovers were united in death.

Fair Juliet awoke entwined within her lover's arms, screaming from the cold flesh that had stiffened around her, banging at the wooden lid of their shared coffin, and wondering how much longer her new life would last.

Cat Russell

Lost and Found (a la The Tempest)

I have never known men like these. Only Caliban, the closest thing I have to a brother, the sharer of my toils, misery, and loneliness. And Ariel…but he is an airy spirit—wise and good but not a man. My father was lost to me long ago, so long, I have but the most distant memory of his passing.

These men are strange. What would they do were they to know that I am here? Ariel suggests caution in my approach, and I will heed the spirit's warning. Caliban runs to his hiding place, scared of newcomers. Has he not a right to be? Look what happened when he welcomed my father. No matter. I will assuage his fear and call him from his hiding place, once I have enough knowledge to determine our course.

My father…Ariel and brother Caliban tell me my father was both the best and worst of men, and I believe it. If I revealed myself to them, would they make me a slave or liberate me from this isle and my loneliness? I ask the spirit, but he only smiles and says that it is my choice.

The storm is so much like the spirit himself, both terrible and beautiful: the lightning forking through the skies like the fires of creation, the roiling grey clouds, the crashing waves that splintered the good vessel to pieces against the rocks, yet none perished…only washed ashore for my inspection, birthday presents for my fifteenth year.

I thank the gods for my Ariel, for without him I would have been like Caliban when I first discovered him, wild and without words for want of education. But Ariel, in gratitude for the freedom my father granted him, raised me, taught me to read, to learn from my father's books and notes so that all the great Prospero discovered was not lost to time, pages left to rot like his body now lying in the cold, cold ground.

I thank the gods for my Caliban, coarse companion though he is. Poor soul. He was not so fortunate as

I, his mother having passed when she trapped Ariel in the tree years before we arrived. Ariel took long to forgive him for that; though to blame a babe for their parent's folly seems cruel, we cannot help where emotion leads us. I helped Caliban learn language, and he helped me in so many ways. We foraged for food together, ate, slept, bathed, hunted, cried, and even embraced when we saw the ship floundering on the stormy sea; Caliban was frightened, but I knew what it meant.

Freedom.

Ariel looks sad, but I do not know why. Can not the spirit that commands the very weather go wherever he wishes? But no, as I look into his eyes of mist, I realize at last that he cannot. He grants me freedom, as my father once granted his, but Ariel's power is forever connected to this island. He knows how I have longed for this ship. But no, he tells me who these strangers are, and oh, how I have longed for these very men to take me from these shores that have been my home so many years.

Ariel has informed me of the workings of the male heart, and though I am unsure how he would know, I trust his knowledge. Men are strange and should be approached with caution, but I spy the instrument of my revenge in the handsome visage of the weeping Prince Ferdinand—soon to be King.

So I will reveal myself to this forlorn prince, this someday king, to one day become his queen. And if my beauty and "innocence" are not enough to ensnare his heart, I have my father's magical arts to call upon. I will use them to repair the ship, enough to carry us to his country, and we will rule together.

As for this prince's king-father and my own treacherous uncle, they both shall languish here as I and my father once did. Unskilled at the magical arts, I wonder how long they will last. My Ariel, my friend, will not help them. In fact, knowing his heart, I suspect they will soon pray for swift deaths.

I smile at the thought.

Vengeance for my loneliness, for my father's death, and a home for Caliban—who will conquer his fear for love of me and follow wherever I go. These are birthday presents from my lovely Ariel, the airy spirit of my youth that I leave behind on these familiar shores.

I have my books. Kind Ariel has bound and brought them to me; all else I leave behind.

Including mercy.

Emilia's Divided Duty (a la Othello)

I can't believe he did it.

I can't believe the bastard did it.

Oh, I know he's capable of villainy; mine eyes have seen the proof, but this?

Not villain by any *man's* standard, no, but by mine. Whoring around with his fellow officers, yet beating me for mere suspicion my eye should wander. Well, why shouldn't it? Cassio *is* a proper man, no mistaking. And whilst he's been known to whore it up with Bianca, he's not betrothed so no real harm.

Charm my tongue? Rather sharpen my tongue to cut like a thousand swords. I would do him harm if I could.

My best friend. So sweet a woman, who saw men's visages in their minds, surprised by jealousy!…if she had only had my experience. How long have I watched Iago passed over again and again for promotion, and yet he is the Moor's ensign! I knew it irked him, a seasoned soldier passed over by an unseasoned youngster, but what of that? Could he not see how lucky he was? All his years of battle do not make up for his lack of education, and strategy is all in wartime.

Had I but known what strategy he practiced, I would not have comforted him.

Oh, what a fool I was.

To think that this man could ever truly love me. To tell myself that the restraints he threw upon me were proof of his great love rather than peevish jealousy of me…like a dog he feared would stray.

To think any man who beats his wife for the slightest offense would ever be man enough to get over envy of his fellow soldier.

To think he would ever love my friends as I do, rather than lust after one and plot the ruination of the other.

For what…spite? A promotion? Like Lucifer, he would rather rule in Hell than serve in Heaven. Well, that can be arranged.

My only regret…it will not bring my lady back.

May his pernicious soul rot half a grain a day, I'll stop that lying tongue of his with my own, then cut him to the quick.

I'll tell him to his face all his plans are come to naught, watch his color drain as all realize *honest* Iago is nothing more than a petty scheming villain. I know where he keeps his dagger; I'll wrest it from its place before he chance can flee, and if he has a heart…

I'll bury my point.

The Quality of Mercy (a la The Merchant of Venice)

The God of Abraham is just and smiles on me.

That this young fool, Bassanio, should come to me to beg a loan of three thousand ducats…for what? For what could he need so great a sum! Oh, I am familiar with Christian extravagance. And though they condemn me for loaning what is mine own, yet they come to me when they have need, saying, "Shylock, we would have monies!" What have I to lose from such a bargain?

What are my risks?

I do not have the total sum today, but Tubal, a worthy man of my tribe, shall loan me the balance. I do not fear him, for I am worth the sum and more in just a little time, as soon as the debt itself be paid or my other ventures return in profit. So there I am safe.

If Antonio, the man Bassanio swears will be his guarantor, pays me the sum, I am well. I am well for the sum plus the interest, the interest on such a sum well pays itself.

If Antonio pays me not, he shall be in my debt. Antonio is a good man. Good, I say, for the money, not good by my reckoning, for he spat upon me the other day for no other reason than I am a Jew. He rails against me and my tribe, he berates me for my usances, and undercuts my livelihood by loaning money gratis.

Yet, the God of Abraham and my fathers has shown me this kindness, shown me this kindness that I might return in kind. I shall have reason to show him mercy where he has shown none, show him reason and goodwill where he has shown unreasoning hatred and cruelty, and thus I may curb his enmity to the betterment of all.

But Christian courtesy also teaches me what Christians expect. They see their own bad dealings in others, and, thinking little of my tribe, Antonio shall not expect such recompense for his past treatment of me. Therefore, I shall show him my humor as well, the better shall my mercy shine should he forfeit the bond.

It'll needs be outrageous.

I have it. A pound of his flesh if he pays not the bond! It will fit his expectations of my cruelty, yet his arrogance shall not suspect a danger. Not that there is a danger. The world must needs drive me mad ere I claim such a forfeit!

No, he's good for the money, I'm sure, more's the pity. If he were to forfeit, 'twould be a merry jest to see the look in his eyes before I pardon him, showing him the mercy he himself is bankrupt.

Oh well, the young fool stands waiting. I will bid him fetch his "friend," though I suspect Antonio wishes for more. Christians are a shameful lot. They cannot even follow their own precepts, yet stand in judgement of others. Very well, I am decided. May the God of Abraham bless us all.

The Art of Necessity (a la King Lear)

"What do you think is the reason for this summons, sisters?" Cordelia gazes at her older siblings, concern etched upon skin too young for wrinkles.

The lines in her sisters' faces make up the difference. Goneril, the King's eldest daughter, views her youngest sister with open contempt, before addressing the middle daughter. "Oh, look, Regan…Daddy's favorite doesn't know what's going on either. At least that's something."

Regan sniffs and glares at Cordelia.

Since their youngest sister had spent her teen years away at school, she was spared the worsening of their father's temperament. Cordelia had remained blissfully ignorant of the tumultuous politics of court and still sees their father as the god of her youth, the doting parent who finds nothing in their world as worthwhile and joyful as her…not even his other two daughters. She is his darling, his sole joy, the child of his old age.

Cordelia ignores them, peeking through the curtain at the throne room filled with courtiers awaiting the King's arrival. She spots two she likes: the Duke of Burgundy and the King of France. Both had petitioned the King for her hand. Will her father announce his decision soon? She quivers with excitement. By night's end, she'll know if she is destined to be a duchess or a queen.

Meanwhile, the older women speak quietly among themselves. Their sister's fate will not necessarily affect them. Their father overlooked their interests from the moment of Cordelia's birth. Oh, he did not neglect to arrange their marriages—that was business, after all, but that's as far as it went.

Thank the gods for that! For all the dotage he bestowed upon his youngest, his older daughters suspected his mind had been going for quite some time. While Cordelia had been spared the rages of his younger days, they were well remembered by Goneril and Regan; the two sisters had clung to each other in fear for as long as they shared his castle. At least *those* rages had been infrequent, directed towards others, and always somewhat logical. Lately though, his actions were more troubling.

Thank the gods they are married and no longer forced to share his roof. Living with a mad man is a dangerous, unpredictable business. Living with a mad king is…well, downright crazy.

What else can they do but bow and acquiesce whenever he deigns to summon them? Better to kiss ass than dirt by incurring his wrath.

While Regan continues staring daggers at their sister, the young girl bent peering through the curtain with barely contained glee, Goneril spares her a look of pity. Poor fool. The little idiot is too stupid to know to play the game. She suspects Cordelia, sooner or later, will be in for a rude awakening.

Cat Guts (a la Much Ado About Nothing)

"Is it not strange that cat guts should hail souls out of men's bodies?" mused the red-bearded Benedict, eying the musician and his companions with disdain. Despite this odd-seeming praise for the violinist's musical prowess, Benedict hid in the bushes studiously avoiding the man, though the other humans strained closer as he sang and played. They were evidently pleased with his performance.

However, sitting quietly behind the bearded Benedict, Edgar the cat was not pleased. Violinists may hail souls from men's bodies with their melodies, but the melody of Edgar's fellow felines must have been less than pleasing when their own souls were ripped to make the strings that Balthasar now played. He may not have gutted the cats themselves, yet he harvested the fruits of their slaughter with his lonely, lovely notes. He represented all of cat-kind's dearest foes.

The cat's yellow eyes narrowed, he unsheathed his claws, readying himself to avenge his fellows.

The song ended, and as the other humans gathered round, the musician clothed himself in false modesty by feebly fending off their praise. However, the red-bearded fellow before Edgar mumbled to himself, "Or was that sheep's guts? I can never remember."

Disgusted with himself for falling for this fool's idiotic chatter, an unholy hissing erupted from Edgar's disparaged soul as he leapt into the air, landing on the back of the unsuspecting Benedict. The man batted wildly at the maddened feline, raving about hanging dogs that howled too much or some such nonsense, but—although insulting dogs never hurt—it was too late. Edgar would have none of it. He sank teeth and claws into the cowering Italian, making an altogether more pleasing music to his own furry ears.

As You Liked It or As You Like It Part 2 (a la As You Like It)

"Father, the seating arrangement simply must be changed."

"Why, Rosalind! Whatever do you mean? The couples are all seated next to each other, as befits an Anniversary dinner—"

"But whose Anniversary, pray you? Nay, not just mine and Orlando's, but others' as well!"

"Yes, of course, my dear. Don't you see? I seated Celia and Oliver across from you."

"But what of Touchstone? And Audrey?"

"They're to have an excellent feast in the adjoining room, just as lavish, I promise you."

"In the adjoining room! You did not seem so hard a year ago."

"Well, it simply isn't proper to have commoners seated at the table with nobility."

"What of the Forest Arden! There you were content to sit alongside the beasts of the forest, and indeed, have your daughter married in the same ceremony as a fool and his lady."

"A wise man does not argue with a god, Rosalind, no matter *what* his rank."

"The god, Hymen, is a rather agreeable sort."

"The god of marriage wished to marry you. I will not quibble with a god about his own business."

"It seems uncivil, somehow, to separate the celebrations now that we are back."

"Then we were, as you so kindly observed my dear, in the forest. Manners in town must needs differ from the forest, and indeed, differ widely from Court."

"What will your friend, Jacques, have to say about

that, I wonder?"

"No doubt he will soliloquize awhile, and then wander off to be melancholy."

"He does love to do that sort of thing, does he not?"

"Yes, my dear, though I fear he may not wander far enough. He's rather fond of our fool."

"Of Touchstone? I had forgot, but mayhaps he shake Jacques from his melancholy."

"Oh no, my dear! For his happiness is more a terror than his melancholy. God save me from his mirth."

"Now, Father, you are not in earnest. I see the curl of your lip and the sparkle of your wit. But come now. What of Audrey and Touchstone? Shall we seat them near Celia and her Oliver?"

"That depends. Has Oliver the patience for it?"

"Dear father, he is, of course, a patient and kind man. How could he be otherwise, when sired by Sir Roland and brother to my dear Orlando?"

"That same brother, whose life he aimed to end, I recall."

"A miracle, I grant you. No doubt, my dearest friend, Celia, tamed his rage with her beauty."

"I should hope so, for her sake. He wooed in haste."

"Give thy thoughts no tongue. You do not suggest—"

"No, my dear. I know your friend to be honest, though I do not trust *his* mind. False face may hide what the false heart doth know."

"Father!"

"So the seating arrangement stays the same."

"I have not agreed to such a thing. What of Silvius

and his Phoebe?"

"The shepherd! I grant you, allowances are made for a licensed fool. It is the nature of his craft to be allowed liberties, but a shepherd—"

"Married by the god, Hymen, in the same ceremony as your own daughter and her friends."

"The god is hardly going to come to the anniversary feast, now, is he?"

"--!"

"Oh, my lord Hymen! Pardon this poor mortal. I did not observe your august presence. Of course, I shall seat them together."

"Lord Hymen, my father and I are grateful for your interest in our humble feast. It doth—"

"Left in a flash, did he not, my dear?"

"That was laid on with a trowel."

"As flies to wanton boys are we to the gods."

"Too true, dear Father. They treat the world as their stage, and they are the stage managers."

"So, my dear, I suppose you shall have your way. All the lovers shall be seated at one table, as they were wed in one ceremony."

"What shall we feast upon? Indeed, for I mean to make merry."

"Cakes and ale, my dear! Venison, and all manner of meat. The sauces shall be rich, and our wit more so."

"What of your brother, Frederick? Will he not dine with us?"

"He is most welcome, as always, in my house."

"Did not my Uncle eschew meat when he vowed a monastic life?"

"He need not eat it. I shall, for my own part, eat a

pound of flesh, for my salad days are well behind me."

"But your melancholy friend, Jacques… Will he not object to the venison?"

"Mayhap my head will ache all evening, and *you* may deal with Jacques! All the world's a stage, indeed!"

"But father, I thought him your dear friend!"

"A friend, my dear, but his philosophy is too much for my mind. Better a witty fool than a foolish wit."

"Then it is a good thing Touchstone and his lady will be seated nearby. His merry wit may counter Jacques' philosophy."

"Rosalind, my dear, send for the apothecary. My head doth ache."

Cat Russell

Kate's Tale (a la The Taming of the Shrew)

Best beware my sting, husband Petruchio.

I've dealt with men, the weaker sex, my entire life. My father is a dolt, my suitors were greedy men only after my dowry, blind to my better parts. I counted myself blessed by their absence. Oh, they call me curst Kate, and I agree…cursed to be surrounded by inferiors, yet doomed to have my fate ruled by them.

My younger sister, Bianca, has tamed men to her will her entire life. My father she wrapped round her little finger as one would spin woolen thread, her suitors waited on her slightest wish, bent themselves into knots for her amusement. But whilst she played their game with pretty words, sly smiles, and the batting of her lashes, I never stooped so low. They were not worth my deceit. They felt the full force of my derision.

Well it is then, dear husband, that you are as mad as me in every sense of the word. A lesser man could not have stood the brunt of my rage, nor held up a mirror to mine own behavior. So though you jested with my father when we first met that I but pretended to oppose you (when I loved you privately), it is now—at least somewhat—true. You are the only one ever man enough to face me.

I have learned from watching Bianca all these years how to twist men's wills to my own. Your madness forces me to be the saner one, but your will is now mine. Your debts will be paid, dear husband, not with my dowry but with Bianca's tears. Therefore, I reverse my behavior, to be ruled by you *in public*—so long as we agree in private. It works better this way, to our mutual profit. Four hundred crowns won from her newly duped husband will go far towards paying all debts.

So, my tale by my tongue, and your tongue is well paid by this wager. Now, get thee to bed, and we'll *both* have our reward.

CREDITS

The following published via the 52/250 A Year of Flash challenge (https://52250flash.wordpress.com/) under the name Catherine Russell:

Gingerbread 2011-05-07
Shell 2011-03-22
What Might Have Been 2010-05-29
The Last Time 2010-09-20
Blood 2010-06-18
Brothers 2010-10-12
A Time to Remember 2011-04-06
Naughty 2011-04-11
The Willow 2011-01-03
All's Fair in War 2010-09-27

The following published via sixminutestory.com via Creative Commons Attribution-ShareAlike 3.0

Wine 2014-12-05
Runaway 2015-01-30
Space-Time to Travel 2015-07-17
Gummies 2015-08-14
Sea Life 2016-07-08
Pest Control 2016-06-17
Fame 2014-02-04
Cat Guts 2015-09-11

The following published via my writing blog (www.ganymeder.com aka catrussellwriter.wordpress.com) for the #FridayFlash twitter challenge:

An Optimist's Journal of the End of Days 2018-01-26
It's Not Easy Being Green 2010-06-25
Wine 2014-12-05
Peaches 2010-10-22
Cigarette 2014-06-13
Smart Tech 2016-08-26
Space-Time to Travel 2015-07-17
Space-Timer 2015-05-29
Panic Attack 2014-06-03

Cat Russell

Gummies	2015-08-14
The Price	2012-04-12
No Man's Land	2009-12-11
Paperweight	2009-12-04
Password	2011-03-17
Ghost Writer (short story)	2015-08-15
The Ring	2015-05-08
The Field Trip	2009-09-04
Collection	2010-09-30
A Match Made in the Heavens	2016-10-07
Where There Be Dragons	2009-12-21
Sea Life	2016-07-08
Trapped	2016-10-21
Hot Librarian	2016-03-15
Quietus	2010-05-01
Pest Control	2016-06-17
Looking Glass	2016-06-04
Cliffhanger (short story)	2017-05-11
Capital Crimes	2016-09-23
Parts of Speech: The Untold Story	2009-03-19
53	2015-02-13
The Mad Scientist	2011-01-27
Life is Hell	2012-06-21
A Little Bit of Sugar	2012-01-05
The Story of the Dandelion	2010-06-04
Mangrove	2015-02-06
Advice to a Young Girl Traveling in the Enchanted Forest	2014-02-26
Snow White Retold	2010-08-13
Sleeping Beauty Retold	2012-08-09
Red Riding Hood Revised	2010-05-21
Goldi-locks 2	2010-01-27
Rumpelstiltskin (as Rumplestilkskin)	2012-02-03
The Witch and the Frog	2010-06-11
Fame	2014-02-07
Three Little Construction Workers	2014-11-14
All Happy Families	2014-08-15
Ishmael	2014-08-08
2014	2014-07-11
They Say When	2014-08-01
The Past is a Foreign Country	2014-09-12
Far Out in the Backwaters	2014-09-19
Tempting Fate	2016-05-12
Lightning Rod Salesman	2012-08-23
The Dogcatcher	2011-08-19
Creation	2017-03-10
The Willow	unpublished

AN OPTIMIST'S JOURNAL OF THE END OF DAYS AND OTHER STORIES

Puck's Surprise 2017-08-02
Pucked Up 2017-08-11
What Really Happened to Juliet? 2012-03-15
Cat Guts 2015-09-11
As You Liked It or As You Like It, Part 2 2017-06-29

Published via other blog/site:

Bread 2011-03-31
https://demonesprit.wordpress.com/2011/03/31/bread/
The Game 2019-09-22 via
www.patreon.com/authorcatrussell
Fairy-be-gone 2010-05 via
Soft Whispers Photo Contest
Super Powered 2019-09-08 via
www.patreon.com/authorcatrussell
Red Riding Hood Revised 2012-04
issue of *Beyond Centauri.*
Dream Guy 2012-02 via
Metro Fiction http://metromoms.net/2012/02/26/dream-guy-by-catherine-russell/

Book Credits:

Multiples of Six (science fiction flash) published in In Context: The Eclectic Works of The Write Stuff Authors Group 2019-11 via
Project 89 Media
Hell of a Job (fantasy flash) published in The Best of Friday Flash: Volume One (anthology) 2010-08
Mirror (fantasy flash) published in Twisted Tales 2016: Flash Fiction with a Twist via Raging Aardvark
Femme Fatale (fantasy flash) published in The Best of Friday Flash: Volume Two (anthology) 2012-10

Miscellaneous/inspired by:

Reclamation inspired by a tweet via Mike Cole 2019-09-24
https://twitter.com/MykeCole/status/1176467864229961728?s=19

About the author

Cat Russell shares her life with her high school sweetheart, their son, and other ferocious creatures in the wilds of Ohio while writing short stories, composing poetry, and learning more about the craft every day.

Her work has been published in *Flash Me magazine*, *Metro Fiction*, *Beyond Centauri*, and the *'Best of Friday Flash - Volume One'* and *'-Volume Two,' the Hessler Street Fair Poetry Anthology: 50th Anniversary*, and *In Context*. Her first book of poetry, *Soul Picked Clean*, published March 2019 by Crisis Chronicles Press.

An Optimist's Journal of the End of Days and Other Stories, is her first collection of fiction.

www.ingramcontent.com/pod-product-compliance
Lightning Source LLC
Chambersburg PA
CBHW070630310726
48982CB00001B/239

* 9 7 8 1 7 3 4 9 4 6 9 0 1 *